INCURABLE

STORIES FROM THE WORLD OF CURE

Edited by

LISA DIANE KASTNER

RUNNING WILD

INCURABLE: Stories from the World of CURE

Text Copyright © 2025 Held by each story's author

Published in North America and Europe by Running Wild Press.

Visit Running Wild Publishing at www.runningwildpublishing.com.

Educators, librarians, book clubs (as well as the eternally curious), go to ww.runningwildpublishing.com for teaching tools.

ISBN (pbk) 978-1-960018-64-9

ISBN (ebook) 978-1-960018-63-2

CONTENTS

Thank you to everyone who believed in these stories, created these stories, and enabled these stories to come to life. Without your belief, none of this could have happened.

Please note, some of the stories may contain foul language. Why? Well, why not?

BLOODLINES

BY JERRY PURDON

A roar lingered in the cool air. A second one followed but cut short, falling into an eerie silence. The trees' bare limbs offered no other noises in the breeze. No more screwing around, this was why he was out in the morning sun. The main thought was to locate the trigger of the noise and track it.

His memory fuzzed and at times played tricks which led to confusion, so he reviewed his primary thoughts often. His focus needed to be maintained. He hated this constant struggle. No matter how overwhelming, he had to ignore it. Thus began his internal fight with why a rabbit had less substance than this search. The little guy was ten pounces away. No, he had to concentrate. He shook the furry meal from his cerebral vision. Besides, he preferred eating in a nocturnal setting as well as his more favored time to roam. He glanced one more time in the direction of the delicacy, stretched and pushed his paws forward as he forged a new path toward the outdated cry.

Very few times in his life, did he need to remember and be more than what he was at this moment. For now, his desire to verify won out. Something else hunted this part of the wild and this beast needed to be stopped. The aberrant kills stood out to everyone. Especially since humans were the targets. He may have similar abilities to the killer but this didn't mean they could kill whoever, whatever, whenever. This predator's behavior had become pronounced for the world to see. Unlike his small hunts which easily blended into the locale.

He came out of the roadside thicket almost trotting onto a corpse, a man with the skin of his neck in shreds. Canines, they always go for the throat. The rich iron smell wafted heavily in the air. Another scent wavered across the grounds. The one he needed to follow as well as another, something more familiar, he stumbled where one of them became strong. A female wolf had recently passed through. He followed. The trail held fresh tracks. They were elongated prints, unnatural, and for those of a two-legged animal were as pronounced as water in the desert. He didn't care about the danger of pursuing. He had to know. This was imperative. Not for rabbits, sunlight, or for a friendly countryside prowl, but for stalking.

He traveled through heavy brush deadened from the heat of summer and lifeless from the cool of the darker season. The winter laden foliage still provided cover and blended with his pelt. He gained speed in the open areas and slowed in the thicker mayhem of tangled vegetation, some dead with the remaining in hibernation.

In no time, he covered plenty of acres. He crossed over to familiar property and was far from where he normally played. The trail altered. Another scent was introduced, intertwined with the first, the canines disappeared. Humans. A clearing had to be near. He skulked the next few steps. His face pushed to the edge of the deadened foliage. There were two. A man and a woman stood by a building, the latter had a blanket placed around the lady and his eyes met those of the man.

Based on the male whispers, the woman peered over her

shoulder. The dried blood on her face was obvious. He recognized many an animal from after they had eaten. She was no different. The fright impulse coursed through his soul as he hoped they only saw something of a feline and nothing of his other self. Her mouth formed a smile. One where the lips stretched and protruded. Her head deformed and with a guttural growl, she took steps toward him.

He retreated into the cover of the landscape blending into all the natural colors. His legs moved to run, tracing along the path from where he tracked her, he leapt over the body, passed the place where the rabbit foraged for food, and arrived from where he originated. His form altered and his awareness returned. One day, at some point, he would forget all these human things and stay with nature.

His car was there. Without dressing, he opened the door and drove off. His mind raced and hoped he had not been pursued or recognized. It would be bad for everyone.

His questions were more about how she managed to get blood on her face and hands. This didn't necessarily make her the killer, but it didn't mean she wasn't one. She could have acted in self-defense or been trying to help.

He stopped his car, took a deep breath, and assessed his memories of the couple. In the most recent election, she became the county judge of their commissioners court, and the man who followed her happened to be her husband. As far as he could tell, the man had never said a word to anyone in public anywhere. He had never seen that man's mouth do more than smile. She was the voice of the two and somehow seeing the man's lips move created an uneasy feeling.

He needed time to piece together this ever-growing puzzle.

His only hope from the encounter was she had not figured him out. He had taken great care to be undetected by her and would observe for now as to answer all the questions. He had to find out the side they represented then this might tell him if she was the killer or not. No matter how creepy her husband was, neither had a murderer's cold hard stare. His mission was successful since he was certain, they were shapeshifters.

* * *

Sheriff Hal Larsen stared at the coroner as she took pictures of the victim. Her short, dark hair wavered in the brief gusts. She assisted his team with certain CSI activities regarding personal injury related crimes, including death. Overall, Meredith was a lot more than a body collector and crime scene investigator, she was his niece.

When her parents passed, many years before, Hal and his remaining sister took it upon themselves to raise the girl. He did most of the fun stuff in coaching her softball and soccer teams. Taking her to concerts she wanted to see either in Lubbock or San Antonio. Whatever she needed, he was there for her when she asked and occasionally when she didn't.

At times, when he watched her, the sting of her mother's death panged his heart. Meredith resembled her mother not only by looks but mannerisms as well. At first he thought his memories made them closer than they were, but within the past few months they had found some old Super 8 film confirming he was spot on with his assessment of how exactly alike the two were.

He was disappointed and excited for her when she graduated with honors with a double major in chemistry and biology. He thought she would wander off into medical school somewhere since that was the plan, but after a year in Europe, she changed her mind. Instead, she went to a forensic study program that eventually led her to becoming a coroner. When she returned, she brought a friend, Anson Geller, who now served as lead detective. Hal couldn't recall the last time he'd seen the man without sunglasses but nonetheless, he served as his right hand in the department. He was glad his niece had good friends.

The cool breeze caught his face, and he realized too many people were around. He kept his hands in the side slit pockets of his brown sheepskin coat. He loved the old thing and had it for over thirty years. An internal debate began about buttoning up the jacket as the cold chilled him. A cup of coffee would do the trick. It bothered him, they weren't savvy enough like the movie cops. No one brought any warm beverages of any kind.

"Rough way to go," she said.

Her words jolted him out of his daydream, "definitely looks like it."

"Any ideas on who this is yet?"

"No wallet or identification so sending pictures down to Austin. Hopefully we can get a facial match... For now, John Doe."

"FBI office?"

"No, a buddy over at DPS."

"Oohhh, high rolling with the Rangers, are we?"

He nodded with a slight smirk acknowledging her sarcasm. This county went twelve years without a murder, and all of the ones under his tenure had been domestic related. One of the worst occurred during his first year as a sheriff when an elderly couple apparently, had enough of each other. At least the husband was done with the wife. The old man cooked for the two except the wife's side of the meals came with an extra dash of metal. From opening cans, he took jagged shards and mixed them into her food. Over the period of months, the fragments broke down in her intestines and she bled out. Unfortunately for the old man, their doctor was a true crime buff and naturally became suspicious.

She ran all types of tests eventually and found the cause. Nonetheless, the older woman succumbed to her injuries. Almost fifteen years went by before another murder and that was two brothers arguing over a game of Risk. They dueled with bats. After a few swings, one connected to the other's noggin' leading to a slow brain swelling death. But the case in front of him was the third gnawed neck in six months.

A Landrover pulled up and since only one existed in the county, he knew it was the judge. No way, they could keep this secret. Too many townies were out and about even late on a Saturday afternoon. She approached the scene as her partner stayed in the vehicle. In her hand she carried a carton of four coffees. He may not trust her, but he liked her style.

"Sheriff," she said with her finger pointing towards the corpse. Her eyebrows non-verbally asked for her to approach.

"Judge, come on over," he said motioning for her to enter the area.

Her perfume reached them before she did. Being down-wind of her, the heavy bouquet of a berry related essence was hard to ignore, but he did. He made sure to not change his facial expression based on the overpowering aroma. Her trap was obvious, and he hid himself well as he did from the moment he met her several years earlier. He now knew, she used a shapeshifter's keen sense of smell to root them out. He allowed a quick nod as a greeting. She handed him a coffee. The warmth radiated in his hand.

Obviously, she was there for information, but he never shared details on any active case. As a habit, he suspected everyone and let little out. Not a peculiar way to work an investigation since the only person he knew for sure didn't commit this murder was himself. As for the rest, they were all suspects, some to a greater degree than others.

"Local?" The judge asked.

"No ID, so we're not sure," Hal said, "but between you and me, I'm not familiar with this individual." Looking at the victim's face, she would already have that kind of news. This casualty had to be an acquaintance of someone in the county. He doubted it was a drive through murder. Even this close to the border, the drug deals and related crimes tended to stay on the other side.

Hal wanted to ask how she found out about the location, but in a small town, everyone tends to be in everybody's business. Probably his own dispatch told her. Everybody liked her, including the longtime families in the area. If she went to Sammie's Cafe during any part of the day then someone most likely offered the details without her even prompting for them. The whole county had knowledge of some part of each crime. They also made up parts of the story to fill in any gaps. Since all department personnel used Sammie's as a break room, staying up to date with what filtered down the grapevine was easy.

"Missing throat," the judge said, "so number three?"

"As far as we know," Hal said.

"I know I said this before," she said, "I'm sorry about Larry."

Larry, the second victim, was his best friend. Someone Hal trusted and used as a sounding board. They had known each other since their military days. Of course, he had a certain ability to change form as did the first casualty. Hal took a breath, "Thanks."

They small talked as the last remnants of the body was moved. Hal maintained a keen eye on his detective, Deputy Gellar, acting as CSI, and made sure every bit of detail from the site was meticulously placed into individual bags while another officer stood with a pad logging the evidence.

His niece thumbed through her notebook. He noted a sudden movement of her arm. It jumped out at him the way a sunrise startles the night. The tremble happened several times, an unmistakable sight. She had the family genes. Though he was no expert in how or when their abilities manifested, to him this seemed a tad late in life to start. His sister assumed it had skipped Meredith. There was always a chance she had a disease, but based on their genealogy, most likely not.

From the car, on the way to the station, Hal made a call. He thought it a bit funny everyone called the place "the station" but really it was an office no bigger than a closet. Dispatch was on the other side of the building with the jail across the street behind the courthouse.

"Hey bro," Olive answered on the third ring.

"Hey sis, have you spoken with Meredith yet?"

"About?"

"The family way."

"No, at this point, I didn't think there would be a need."

"Might rethink that." He proceeded to tell her about the tremor and what they had believed dropped from the family tree or at least skipped a generation. They shared ideas on how to break the news to their niece as well as guide her. The guidance, according to Olive, would be more of an indoctrination.

* * *

Once he hung up with his sister, he decided to take a detour and grab something at Sammie's. With night already upon them, he was certain the dinner crowd would be at capacity. All the booths crammed against the windows and wall would be filled. It didn't matter to him, there always seemed to be a place at the counter. He took his favorite spot knowing that from the chrome-plated, green and white stools, overhearing conversations from the nearby tables and the bar was as easy as breathing. He quickly noted that too many words floated around about the latest corpse. Sammie approached him wearing her usual smile along with her green button down shirt displaying her name embroidered in white cursive letters above the left pocket.

"Hal," Sammie said with a nod.

"Sammie."

"Usual lunch or dinner?"

"Neither, how about some soup."

"French Onion?"

"Jordan's?"

Sammie allowed a quick smirk. "Yes and she's still in the kitchen."

"Would love some."

Jordan, Sammie's daughter, had escaped West Texas rural life. She became an actual chef in the Big Apple and after a few years, grew tired of the hustle and bustle that the city life offered. No matter her reasons, all the locals were glad she returned bringing some outstanding recipes with her. Plus, she had been Meredith's best friend since primary school. He couldn't remember the last time he saw her but was glad she was working at this moment.

"Shouldn't you be lookin' for a killer," a deep baritone voice said.

Hal recognized this asshole's voice, Tom Hawley, the local contrarian to anything sensible. The sheriff didn't bother to look over at its originator, "if I look now then I'm looking at you."

The man huffed and left the counter. Hal stared at the vacated spot. Between them held a shiny napkin dispenser and the realization he needed to release a statement. He wasn't ready. Maybe he could say something about an animal so people wouldn't fear their neighbor, but it might be bad to have them relax. Still, he had to grab a couple of more days. Besides, he had an idea on who to follow, and either they might lead him to the perpetrator or be the killer themselves.

Sammie delivered his soup in a ceramic bowl. The strong aroma of pepper, thyme, onions, and Gruyere cheese greeted his senses causing him a slight bit of joy. Sammie patted his hand.

"Hang in there," she said.

"Thanks," he said, "and thank Jordan as well."

"You're welcome, and of course," her rouge accented cheeks were more pronounced than usual. She grabbed a cloth to start cleaning the back of the counter.

Hal consumed his soup. With every bite, he wanted to peer over his shoulder to see how many scrutinized him as he sipped from his spoon. Normally, he would have eaten slower but the back of his neck felt like a movie screen. They needed some assurance, and he needed to give them some.

It didn't take long to empty the bowl. He left more than enough cash for the meal and tip, then stood and surveyed the room. All eyes were on him, and he spoke to them, "Be here Monday morning at nine, and I'll have an update on the happenings today as well as progress on finding the perpetrator."

* * *

Hal sat in his handmade wooden chair. It was strategically placed near his front door yet off center of the porch to his ranch style house. It took him thirty-two attempts before he perfected one for his build, and he enjoyed it every moment he could. Even in the cool of winter, he preferred to rest on his porch and take inventory of the day. The weight of an item in his jacket pocket felt like a lump in his chest instead of something heavy and concealed by clothing.

A fire from an old cast iron wood burning oven provided plenty of warmth, perfect for cold evenings and cooler mornings. It was positioned slightly behind him between his chair and another. He hoped he had enough wood chopped for the night. The pile appeared to be less than what he remembered. Someone had offered him a small fortune for the hunk of metal a few years back, but he never had much use for money. What he had was enough for him, and whatever he had left would eventually go to the young woman currently walking up the steps. He expected her and had readied himself for the conversation she might need. To Hal, her Avenged Sevenfold concert t-shirt culture clashed with her western hat, jeans, and boots.

"Hal?"

"Mere," he responded with a casual tone. He had always shortened her name which became okay for him to use but if anyone else attempted it then that individual would be harshly reprimanded. He only used the shorter version when they were alone. He would hate to have led some poor soul along the folly of using her nickname. "You asking as if you aren't sure it's me or do you have another question?"

She giggled as she approached him and sat next to him. Her steps stuttered as though the weight of the world rested on top of her. Her normal upbeat manner was somewhat subdued, so he assumed Olive had the talk.

"Take a load off," he said.

"I guess you know why I'm here."

"Possibly."

She sighed. He loved that she hated his coyness, but he also always wanted her to be direct and come out with what was on her mind. If you can't trust family then you probably would have some trouble with having confidence in anyone. He never wished that for her. Knowing how some families were, plenty of people had big time faith in family issues. For Hal, everything started with trust.

"She told me some crazy shit," Meredith paused, took a deep breath, "Like, I'm a werewolf."

"And you believed her?"

"Of course not," she said, "Olive mentioned how you noticed my tremor then she went on about the family legacy. I thought she was losing it. I gave her the benefit of the doubt with the possibility of the onset of dementia."

"But..."

"She demonstrated..."

He laughed. The first time he saw Olive turn had terrified him for months. She was ten years his senior and he was an early teenager. Their father had taken their other sister shopping for an art project at school, leaving them alone. Olive was on the phone with a soon to be ex-boyfriend and she became angry, transforming on the sofa while she sat next to him. It was also when he first learned the family secret.

"And though it scared me, well somehow I felt empowered. At least my issue is not some deadly disease."

"I can understand that."

He reached into his jacket, retrieving a long, heavy necklace. It felt great to get it off his chest. Some of the stone beads were metallic such as gold, silver, and copper while others were green, red, yellow, and blue. All had unrecognizable lettering on each side.

"Pick that section of red stones," he said, "and run your fingers over them."

Her posture tensed as she sat straight, her eyes wide, staring ahead.

"Go on, do it again," he said, "except this time say the words that come to mind."

With no hesitation, she ran her fingers across the symbols again. This time she spoke.

"nainaṁ chindanti śastrāṇi nainaṁ dahati pāvakaḥ na cainaṁ kledayanty āpo na śoṣayati mārutaḥ"

She dropped the beads and turned toward him, "what the hell was that?"

"You tell me."

Tears spilled from her eyes, "Something about the soul not being destroyed by the elements."

"Close, and a great start."

"I feel different."

"I'm sure you do."

"Listen, I went to the doctor..."

"... and they said you had a disease because they spotted genetic mutation and they always go to a disease, usually Huntingtons, but they have no clue. Fortunately, you didn't pick a doctor who has the same condition as us."

"Why?"

"Not gettin' into the details just yet. Not until you run through the necklace a few more times. There's a ton to discuss but for now, you need to go inside, make yourself comfortable and keep running your fingers over the red section."

She reached for his mug to take a drink, glanced down, and returned it to the table.

"That's just coffee," she said.

"Yep, based on what we need to cover tonight, I altered my usual routine."

She nodded and went into the house as he took a sip from his mug. He sat by his fire enjoying the peace of nature and giving her time to adapt. Then he would assist her once she was ready. Knowing Meredith was always an overachiever, it wouldn't take her long. Plus with what was going on around them with the killings, she needed to come up to speed and fast.

* * *

His paws padded the dirt of the rough terrain. The world was lit by the stars, giving him plenty of light. This deep into the dark hours, sounds were clear, uninterrupted. The current task was to monitor and remember but there was so much to see like other creatures, how the light reflects off the ground, and how the shadows blend with plants. He was never sure he would go back. But he knew he had to return. He did this for her.

Scents of something recently killed carried in the air and as he approached something grunted a few steps ahead. He could view anything from afar, only the obstacles needed to be removed. Once he passed some more of the underbrush he came into a clearing and stopped.

Across the opening were two unnatural beasts. The judge's essence carried in the breeze, and he recognized her. The other he assumed was her husband. They were mating near what was left of their meal. Something that used to be a deer but ripped to shreds and partially consumed. He couldn't help to think of what a tasty treat it must have been.

However, he didn't want to be too close to the creatures, mating or not, his scent would carry over to them, and he had no desire to end up ripped apart like the carcass. He wanted nothing to do with them other than verifying their activity and concentrate on catching a killer. He pondered for a bit if he should wait to see what they did after but he figured from their hunt, meal consumption, and coupling, they would probably sleep. So he returned to where he started his nighttime stroll.

* * *

Hal performed his usual morning routine which was similar to his evening routine. He sat on the porch with the roaring oven and since it was dawn, drank coffee. Meredith hadn't risen yet. He expected questions, but she kept at her stones for a long while before collapsing. As far as he could tell, she didn't change.

The wooden door opened and she came out wearing one of his coats over her yesterday clothes. She parked her own cup of coffee next to his on the table between them. Her expression plain. They relaxed in silence for a few minutes.

"Question?" She asked.

"Answer."

"The necklace was my great grandmothers?"

"Yes, her name was Darshwana. She met your great grandfather, Havelock, in the UK where they married and eventually immigrated to the US."

She chuckled, "I know their names, and I get this ability from her?"

"Yes and the necklace was hers as well as your mothers."

"You don't need it?"

"No, I have my own. All of these relics get passed from one generation to the next. The rest are in a fireproof safe under the floorboards."

"Okay."

They sat in silence drinking their coffee. Though the cups chilled quickly in the brisk morning air.

"You want another cup?" She asked.

"Not at the moment, but I would like to know of any

visions."

"I had plenty, and the dreams came in waves. I know I am Rakashi and we are an ancient line."

"Yep, because the past teaches the present. We understand the natural lore from my grandmother more than our grandfather. We have genes from both bloodlines."

"I have lots of questions," she said, "and yes, I dreamt of being a monster, a cat, a bird, and a snake."

"Yep, your mom could do all of those."

"This scares the shit out of me."

"Good, it should."

"What about you?"

"I'm not like you, I only have one."

He hoped she didn't follow up on his statement. His father always viewed him weaker than his sisters, but for him it wasn't about options. His shifting experience centered on actually becoming something other than himself. He liked leaving humanity and joining nature. It was real. His journey was never for personal gain, or getting the upper hand on someone. His change, when he performed it, was to embrace the world around him.

"Only one?" she asked.

So much for hope. He didn't want a philosophical discussion nor did he want to sway her in the art of changing. She needed to discover her own path from her ancestors.

"Yep, I was never as strong as my sisters."

They enjoyed the morning a bit longer, went in to cook breakfast, and he continued to answer her queries. Meredith took to her new lineage fast. Much quicker than he ever did, and according to Olive he had never reached his full potential.

Meredith practiced her stones through the course of the

day. Her incantations were clear and concise. From what he overheard, it was as if they were already memorized. She shifted a couple of times and from what he was told, retained her memories from each step. Again, it was something he struggled with and it took him years. He still had recall issues. She had it down in a day. He recognized she was talented but had no idea of how much until now.

* * *

A standing room only crowd had taken over Sammie's. The sea foam green and white checkered tile was covered with many types of shoes which beheld the feet of curious minds. Hal used no microphone or bullhorn as his voice carried over the small town multitudes. Their faces all faced him. A captivated audience and more than half would add on to whatever he said. They would take the truths he handed out and shred them of any actual beneficial information. Still, he said he would give an update, most of which would be the same facts found in any police report concerning leads and helpful tips from the community. Everyone stood when he spoke.

This little show offered enough until the next victim came forth. For now, the substantial fact was for the perpetrator to be aware he was a suspect. He added bits about good old fashion detective and police teamwork with the community. Many heads nodded. He worried there would be an 'Amen' or two. This grouping had that kind of feel.

"With that said," he continued, "the killer has made the attacks appear as something done from a wild animal or one well trained. All three victims had their throats removed by what looks to be from the mouth of another animal, like a large feline or canine. DNA tests have come back negative in this area." He searched the room for the judge and stared right at her, "So the killer is human or in this case, humanoid, since these attacks are inhumane. Any questions?"

The place remained quiet for a few seconds but as always, there's, at least one.

"I have a question," the judge held up her hand ever so slightly with her fingertips just above her head, "it sounds as though you know who the killer is at this point."

"We have a general suspect but are still going through due process," he answered.

"But for the safety of the community," she paused, her eyes raised with concern, "why not nab him now?"

"If we do not complete our process and pick up the suspect earlier than planned then we may have followed a mislead, and the true suspect will then kill again. So, when we nab the dirt-bag, you will know for sure we have enough evidence for a conviction. We will leave no reasonable doubt."

"Fair," she said and as the crowd turned back to Hal, she allowed an ever so slight wink.

* * *

The rest of the day went by fast due to a vehicle fatality. He hated when someone died and hated it more when he had to supervise the scene.

So far, other than family and the judge along with her husband, he knew of no other shapeshifters. The first victim was a long time rancher. He had no known next of kin but was active with Hal's brother in law, David, in shape shifting organizations. David and Olive had taken sides, something he wished they hadn't done. He was all for having ideals, but when they became involved in enacting those thoughts forcibly onto others, well that crossed the line. He prayed his sister wasn't involved in this, but in the end, the law must be upheld.

Nonetheless, someone of their ilk was behind all of this, so all shapeshifters needed to be under surveillance. At some point, one of them would slip up.

As he assisted deputy Gellar with investigating the vehicle fatality, Hal's thoughts raced with concerns about the judge's involvement. He had to watch her more and confirm her motives. Blood on her hands was not an indictment, but it didn't mean a squeaky clean image either. Assumptions in any investigation led to a mistrial. One had to get all the facts, and he found it peculiar there never seemed to be enough DNA evidence to link anything. Even Lycanthrope's left behind physical proof.

Tonight he would have to prowl.

* * *

He darted through darkness across the acreage of those who he needed to understand. His paws enjoyed the run. The breeze rushed past his whiskers giving him a partial thrill for his nightly stroll. He loved being a lynx more so than anything else.

The clearing where the beasts consumed their hunt appeared empty causing him to track further into the land. The evening was still early. Plenty of people could still be out, including the lady he hunted, but as he closed on her house, there was something familiar out front. He recognized it, a jeep. It should not be at this place.

The site caused him to pause. It still didn't quite register, but it did. His target may be harming someone he cared about. A pang of danger for the young one inside. She's just a cub and should not be there. These people were hunters. The girl inside associating with them did not make sense.

He trotted onto the porch. There were no open blinds. The doors were all shut. Even the sidelights had coverings. He sensed her inside. She seemed content. He went to the side yard and watched the door.

Without time he waited. The distant sounds from the road lessened. The night grew later. When she emerged, relief filled him.

She walked out alone with no one at the door, and strolled to her car. As she reached for the handle, she paused and peered back at him. His heart pounded as he froze at his possible discovery. She did not pursue him. Instead, she hopped in and drove off.

He circled the home once more and left. His thoughts became more human and centered on doing something different.

* * *

As per the morning ritual, Hal sat on his porch with coffee at his side as the sun broke through the dark revealing the lightest shade of blue. He missed his buddy, Larry. They had great porch discussions, most in the evening but occasionally the morning started out this way. Now solitude was his only friend, the nature of things taking to their form as the day dawned, teaching him something new. It amazed him to be able to sit and witness how animals first start their day, how birds chirped before a ray of light hit the sky, how a busy day got before the break from night. Sometimes he transformed and played along for a bit. He wondered if the first settlers who worked the land ever took the time to appreciate these things. He imagined those that did, had better crops since they were in tune with all the things around them.

This Tuesday morning was no different than any other weekday morning until a car pulled up and his niece headed toward him.

"Hal," she said.

"Mere," he didn't want to seem anxious about what she had to say, but he was. His thoughts shifted to hoping she'd explain where she was and why. "Twice in a few days. You okay?"

"Well, the judge invited me over last night for dinner with her and her husband." She paused as if searching for the right words. "The woman wouldn't let the case go. She asked about how the attacks looked like a wild animal and kept digging for details." Meredith looked at Hal, "so I told her a lynx. It was made to look as though a lynx attacked the victims."

"Why a lynx?"

"Why not? I couldn't say werewolf. And I'm glad I told her a type of feline since I saw one when I left her house last night."

"Really? I didn't know we had any around here."

"Apparently so."

He sipped his coffee, "you want a cup?"

"Sure."

She went inside as Hal continued his appeal to nature. He found it interesting she had the senses to see a lynx at night. Her skills were getting honed and fast. She had to be more powerful than Olive, and he wondered if her father had the gene. That fact had never been mentioned. Meredith brought him away from his thoughts as she returned.

"How's your incantations coming along?" He asked.

"Great, I can do almost all of them without the necklace now."

"That's quick."

"It feels natural. Like something I was missing had been found."

"No more tremors?"

"None."

He quizzed her on transformations and the family legacy; she understood it all. She was bright, but it shocked him how fast she mastered her new knowledge. He didn't want to ruin their chat, but he needed to make her aware.

"I love both of my sisters, yet they were on different sides of our political spectrum."

"That's direct."

"Do you know me to be any different?"

"Not really."

"And while I'm being direct, don't let Olive and David lead you into their crap."

"Okay."

"Good," it was the first time he showed any relief in months. His smile was a give away. Still, she needed information, "Also, be careful of the judge."

"The judge?"

"Yes, she is a Lycan for sure."

"The perfume," she laughed.

"Yes, that unique blend of natural aromas that trigger heightened senses. And she can tell by the reaction if you have more than a neutral human sense of smell."

"That stuff hits you as soon as she gets out of her car. It's like she wears ten coats of Deep Woods Off or something like limburger cheese, just a strong scent coming around the corner before she does."

They both laughed. Tears strolled down their faces.

"Her new nickname, Deep Woods Off," he said, "but seriously be careful. She's baiting either us or someone else. I don't know for sure if she is the killer but if she isn't, she is looking as hard for them as I am."

"Why not just arrest her?"

"No hard evidence. I really don't think she is the killer, but probably knows who it is."

"Husband?"

"I don't think so, but I have eyes on them."

"Cat's eyes?"

He chuckled and ignored her question. They chatted more about the case but nothing Hal hadn't already thought of or was in the process of trying. He just had to bide time and wait for the judge or whoever the killer was to mess up.

The morning blew by as did lunch at Sammie's. Now Hal sat at his desk staring at some pictures and reports. The lack of DNA made no sense. He was aware Meredith took extra time with some samples, yet the state had returned nothing. Today, she proposed the idea that maybe the state wasn't a safe place due to sample sabotage on the opposite side.

He hadn't thought about it that way. His phone buzzed with Olive calling.

"Hey sis."

"Hal," he detected a bit of hysteria in her voice, "David hasn't come home. He went to the store this morning around nine."

He checked the time, it was almost two. To say he was worried was an understatement.

"I'll look for him."

The entire department, around twenty deputies, combed the county. Hal had found David's empty Dodge Ram by the roadside. Nothing appeared amiss and the truck could still operate so something caused him to stop. Chances were, David knew the kidnapper but this was different from the earlier incidents. The bodies of two victims were found at their residence and both lived alone. The third victim had the misfortune of entering their county, but Hal began to think the perpetrator wasn't strong enough to take on Olive and David. A simple approach to remove one at a time instead of going at both. It was obvious Meredith and Olive were in danger.

Hal went to see Olive and console her. Meredith was there. Her disheveled appearance caught him off guard. Her tired eyes were older than what they had been. Hal bet she was working too hard at mastering her skills. He realized they were all he had. He could not search for David and protect them at the same time. He was glad Deputy Geller came with him.

"Geller." Hal said.

"Right here, sheriff," Geller said.

Hal paused as he caught a view of his deputy. They were inside a house and although it was a sunny day outside, the man still had his sunglasses on and for some reason it seemed a bit much. He shook his head, "I need you to stay with them," Hal said and stared at Olive, "non-stop."

"Hal," Meredith said, holding her hands up.

"No," he said, "I don't want anything to happen to either of you."

"We can handle it," Olive said with an almost guttural growl.

Hal searched his sister's eyes and nodded.

"I'm sure you can, but I'm not taking chances. Anson is Meredith's friend, and I can trust him to protect you both with his life."

He stated his position and believed Olive would have normally protested, but she was a bit lost without David. Geller staying with them allowed him to continue his quest for his brother-in-law.

"I'll stop by when I can," Hal said.

He didn't wait for an answer but walked out the door. He

couldn't barge into the judge's house, but staking out her place was happening, starting now.

* * *

He stalked outside her door. His paws silent on the ground, but his mind raged within wanting to be inside performing a thorough search of the grounds. He hated being this way. It was unnatural. Instead of playing in the night, he had to find someone. At the moment, he stood his ground and waited. There was no significant movement, but they were home, he sensed them. Lights were on, but they huddled in a room with the blinds drawn. The person he had to find was not anywhere near.

He went around to the other buildings where they kept the autos and other equipment but picked up no familiar scents. No matter how many times he walked the place, it stayed the same.

He ignored something curious near a brush pile. Another four-legged creature smaller and something fun to play with. He pushed the thought away. After what seemed an eternity, the lights went out. He waited, no doors opened. No new odors. Nothing. It was quiet. Almost too quiet.

Tired and with nothing, he went back the way he came.

* * *

Hal answered his phone. Nothing new on David. Olive and Meredith had a restless night, but they were okay. Geller was still on watch.

After his call, he thumbed through a recent report on the background of the judge and her husband. Nothing stood out. She inherited a lot, and he made it big in investment banking right out of school. So they both left the urban areas for something more rural. No kids. It's not clear why, but he assumed probably one of them had an issue.

Hal had come across several murderers in his time. Whether a serial killer or an occasional one, the same stale eye stare. They had no remorse, were ruthless when they lashed out, and they acted again and again based on their convenience. The judge had warm eyes. Her husband, though strange, maintained a pensive expression as he always observed those around him. They both lacked a malicious look.

Even as a shapeshifter, if one kills often enough their face will wear the sin. They didn't have it. Of course, they could be complete psychopaths, but he didn't believe that. As a simple hunch, he didn't think it was them but he needed more, he needed physical evidence to point out the true murderer.

The other part to solving this, was his desire to get Olive and Meredith out of town before something happened to either of them. He couldn't bear the thought of losing them. If something did happen, well he pushed that thought away. No more dancing around, he had to act fast.

As agreed upon, he met Olive, Meredith, and Geller for lunch at Sammie's. Olive wanted the world to know she wasn't hiding, and she damned sure didn't want the killer/kidnapper to think she was scared in any form or fashion. No, she wished them to make another move. As a precaution, she even kept a Bowie knife on her. Though she said she didn't need it but still wore it slightly to the side in the small of her back. She said after a while, it was as unnoticeable as wearing underwear.

As they conversed, Hal maintained being vigilant. Nothing unusual to spot. His next step was going out to drive around until it was time for him to go back home and get ready for another late night stakeout.

They all ate well. An impending doom crept over Hal as they finished. No matter how much he thought of happier things, the sensation stayed strong as though it was a true warning bell.

When he left, he hugged them both as if it would be for the last time. He stared at the three of them as they were getting into Geller's vehicle and as they drove off as soon as they were secured.

* * *

Almost as the night before, his paws padded the dirt below him as he hid behind a wall of brush. He concentrated on why he was there. Like the preceding night, a rodent crossed not far away. His memory needed to hold. It was all the same, except the woman stepped outside, for a brief bit, to smoke. He knew what she smoked but couldn't think of the name of it. She was only outside for a few minutes but the smell was an affront to all his senses.

Though he was far enough away, she created such a fog with each exhale, so much of one, the blood sucking insects would not go near her. Once she finished, she went inside. The lights went out and their windows were open. He traipsed to the other buildings, after he heard their private sounds.

He paced as he waited. The moon changed positions several times through the course of the night. Nothing occurred. As he went around the house, he searched for scents and nothing new came about.

Tired, he padded down the path from whence he came though it was getting to the point he didn't want to go back. However, the time was late and he had other things to do. He wrestled inside while struggling to remember he would need to become a man to do them in.

* * *

The unfading, overwhelming dread consumed him. He interrupted his way home to drive past Olive's. The front of the house appeared fine. Olive was much stronger than him. When she transformed to the canine side, she unleashed a ferociousness which scared the hell out of him. For whatever reason, his strength or other abilities were never close to that of either sister.

He sighed as the dark cloud still oppressed him. The last time he felt such a thing was when his younger sister died. He was in the military at that time and was stateside so he was able to call them everyday. It started a week before her death so this just happened yesterday, maybe he had a week to solve the whole ordeal.

Hal put the truck into gear and drove off. He needed a bit of rest. His body recharged fast and a few incantations later then he would be fine. However, sleep would come for him at some point, and he would disappear for quite a few days. His body always paid the piper. It was just a matter of when.

* * *

With only a couple hours sleep, Hal woke before sunrise, exhausted. Cleaned up a bit, dressed and went over to Olive's. She should be up sometime around seven. No lights were on, so he waited until the blue started breaking down black.

Passing the time, he swiped through song selections on his phone. He never had much use for television but he did listen to a ton of music. All types, and this morning, he put on some light jazz. The dread was heavy on his shoulders, he hoped something peppy would change his feelings. Even after a couple of songs, the oppression felt stronger. This was something he could not ignore.

He had to move Olive and Meredith to a safer location. This would require a favor or two but hiding them away in a neighboring county while still keeping tabs on them was priceless. Olive could most likely handle herself but she could go down attempting to protect Meredith. His niece had been adapting fine to their ancestry, but she still wasn't ready for combat. No one ever was even after lots of training. A surprise or two always existed.

The half dark sky evaporated, and the remaining stars faded into the blue. Olive's lights were still not on. Ten 'til seven and something should be happening. Unless they both stayed up all night.

Hal turned off his Jeep and headed up to the house. The quiet stoked his fears as he took his key out to unlock the door. He didn't need one, it was slightly ajar. He pushed it open. Pieces of furniture and shattered glass littered the living room floor. No sign of Olive, Meredith, or Geller.

He took a cautious step in and heard nothing so he continued into the kitchen. Empty and clean so he went back through the main room and down the hallway. Holes punctured the walls and pieces of furniture were thrown everywhere. He went further to where Meredith was supposed to sleep. Her room was fine with the bed made. In the next guest bedroom, part of the wall was missing which created an additional opening into Olive's bedroom.

Her room looked as though a bomb had demolished it. Still no one was inside the room so he went toward the master bath. Two pale legs jutted from behind the door. Ones he recognized as belonging to his sister.

Tears trailed his face. He committed to entering all the way to grasp the full scene. The totality of the debris, the bruised and broken body of a loved one settled in once he absorbed it all. He was surprised Olive's head was still attached due to the amount of flesh ripped away from her neck. His sister's eyes fixated on the ceiling but the last thing she saw was the killer.

"Mere?" Hal asked.

Something was alive near him. It was as if its life-force gave off the biggest beacon in history. Someone was near, and he hoped to God it was Meredith.

He moved toward the closet. The door had been smashed. Only shards and splinters clung to door hinges. He entered and searched. Meredith was under a pile of what used to be hanging clothes. She wore blood as though it were makeup. It covered her face, neck, hands, and her nightshirt. Her bewildered eyes lacked focus. It must have been one hell of a fight.

He picked Meredith up, carrying her out past her aunt's corpse and down to where Meredith should have been sleeping. The young woman was coming to and Hal wanted her on the bed before she became fully awake. She mumbled.

"Olive can fight," she said, her whisper barely audible.

"Yes, she can." His sister was a badass. Both of his sisters were total warriors, strong and gifted but look what it got them. One dead in a car accident and the other dead in her bathroom. Neither of their husbands found. Both had disappeared. He shook his head at how similar their lives were between the two though they stood on opposite sides, when it came down to blood, no way one would hurt the other. Family was too thick for that.

"Where's Geller?"

"Thrown out a wall. I haven't made it out to check on him."

Meredith had some head injuries, that much Hal could tell. He had his cell out and called it in. His dispatch would take care of the normal things, He would find who was behind this from Meredith and deal with them.

* * *

Meredith finally came around. Between the paramedics and the doc, they gave her fluids and said her injuries were nothing more than bruises and exhaustion. He wanted her to go to the hospital in another county but she refused. It was pointless to argue with her and she started to work the scene of which everyone said a big whopping no to, so she sat on the sofa making suggestions.

Geller relaxed next to her with his head bandaged. He stared off in the distance. All he said to Hal was sorry. The man took the job to heart and Hal appreciated that, but neither were able to identify their attacker.

From what they said, both had fallen asleep on the couch and they awoke to a battle. Apparently Geller had seen some transformations but wasn't coming clean about it. Olive or David always took care of this type of memories for people. Hal lacked an answer for that at the moment.

The rest of Hal's crew processed the scene which took most of the day. The judge never stopped by nor did she call and that's because it was obvious who the killers were. There was no reason to play coy. The judge or her husband whomever did it had to be incredibly strong to take out Olive but they missed Meredith probably because they had the shit kicked out of them too. Which means they should have some type of battle scars.

All the samples were sealed. This looked like a battle between werewolves and this was one hell of a fight. She must have been swinging something heavy which would be why Olive used her strength. However, all the extra crime scene rhetoric was at a minimum, what he assumed was out of respect to him.

His team brought him, Meredith, and Geller some food. The two ate well, but Hal did not. A huge empty pit had opened inside him, no meal would fill. Exhaustion began to take its toll.

Around the middle of the afternoon, he took Meredith and Geller back to his place and put her in his room. He gave Geller a slug filled shotgun and told him not to ask questions only to shoot. It was time for Hal to go confront the judge. This shit stopped now.

All that mattered for the moment was his last relative. He had to protect her and end this nonsense. Why everyone had to pick sides was beyond him.

Except this time, he needed to take matters into his own hands. He couldn't allow for Meredith or himself to be the next victim. He did not like this tact but had no choice. This last remnant of family required protection, and sometimes you had to go to war for such a thing.

* * *

He answered the knock at the door with a pistol in hand. The judge stood on the other side. He hated the thought of even using a gun, but unloading all seventeen rounds into her seemed like a sound strategy though it might land him in prison. The urge to fire away grew as she remained in front of him.

"Sheriff," she said.

"Judge," he answered while visualizing her death.

"I," she started, "like you, believe in the rule of law. I'm not a murderer."

"What makes you think you are a suspect?"

"The lynx that keeps appearing around my house every night. I can smell your ass within fifty feet."

"A heightened sense of smell."

"Like most, except stronger than a lot of the bloodlines, and I can pickup a feline stench as far away as the next county."

He maintained eye contact, no flared nostrils, no brow twitch, her face remained calm and sincere. Still, too convenient, he didn't believe her.

"Who's the killer?" he asked.

"I can't..."

"...can't tell me."

She nodded.

"What about the rule of law?" He asked with a raised eyebrow.

"This is extremely delicate, and I think the attacker should tell you."

"No one turns themselves in."

"I don't think they'll turn themselves in but they will come forward."

"Judge, I'm done playing games."

Hal was going to slam the door, but instead he exited. She stepped back a few steps and left the porch. Her husband walked over to her.

"Two against one?" Hal asked.

"We are not against you," the judge said.

Footsteps approached the entryway behind him. He didn't want his niece anywhere near the judge and instantly wished she wasn't at his house.

"Meredith," Hal said, "You need to go inside and send Geller out."

"I can't," she said, "not until you hear the truth."

"Which is?" He asked.

She hesitated, "I can confirm, the judge is not the killer of anyone or David's kidnapper."

Hal maintained his view of the judge and her spouse. If she wasn't the murderer then her man had to be it. Of course, the husband stood stoically by the judge without so much as a facial twitch or expression of any kind. Her man had to be the servant of the misdeeds carried out under her orders.

"So her husband?" Hal asked.

"No," Meredith sighed.

He turned towards his niece. Her demeanor reminded him of her mother's. One of caring, warm eyes, except hers had something other than warmth. A shiver trickled down his body as a light dawned inside about a possibility he had ignored. He needed the judge, who stood off his porch with Silent Bob, to come forward with the truth. If it was not them, he was unsure if he wanted to find out more.

"It was me," Geller said from behind Meredith, "I did most of the killing along with Jordan."

"Jordan?" Hal asked in the air. He could not fathom both his niece and the other young woman to be killers. He shook his head in denial but Geller's eyes told the truth.

"I'm sorry about Larry," Geller continued, "but he was too close to David and found out about us."

The emptiness inside Hal grew. He didn't think it was possible for there to never be DNA evidence after such thorough searches. The improbability of it all should have alerted him. They were scrubbing their own crimes. Still there's no way Meredith murdered Olive or was a party to it. She would never betray her family.

"Why?"

"My dearest and loving uncle killed my parents, as in your sister, my mother."

"Bullshit... Olive would have never allowed it."

"No, Hal, she didn't just allow it. She authorized it. This

was due to my father's pure blood lineage and the fact he stood against The Righteous Group that Olive was aligned with. She ran the show and David was her muscle."

"No."

"Yes," Meredith tossed a leather journal that landed at Hal's feet, "I marked the page where they made the decision. It is written in my uncle's handwriting. I found it during the summer between my junior and senior year while home from college. I couldn't believe it."

"You shouldn't. Probably something the judge here planted, so you could join her side."

"No, I met the judge when I went to Sweden, and she decided to move here to guide me. She didn't want anyone killed. She wanted evidence but they began to discover who we were."

"This doesn't make sense."

It did add up. Hal wanted to continue his ignorance and not face the truth even though it slapped him in the face about his niece taking on what was left of his family. All of Olive's circle was taken out by the one he cared the most about. The one he wanted to protect.

"It's all in David's book," Meredith said, "and he was meticulous with his communications to some asshole named Chago. I went to Europe and found Birger. He taught me about your grandparent's and my father's lineage. I faked the tremor and you gave me access to the rest of my heritage."

"Father?"

"You didn't know? He was Scandinavian royalty and with that comes a lot of pure blood. Mix that with my great-grandmother's and according to Birger you get a super me. With my great grandmother's beads, I've grown so much."

"So I'm next, is that it?"

"Not at all," her voice took on a pleading tone, "you only

desired law and order along with a trusting family. You never picked a side, and you never wanted this power. You are a good and decent man. I had to come clean and so did the judge."

"Did you have to kill Olive?"

"She started asking pointed questions, she changed and attacked me. She put it all together and once she knew I took care of David, she lost her shit."

"You killed David?"

"He murdered my father and mother. I left him in pieces where no one else would find him. The only other one was at the roadside. He met with the judge and myself, then started a fight."

Hal glanced at the book by his feet, shook his head. He had trouble digesting her words. She was involved in something he spent a lifetime avoiding though it was always around him. The one supposed to be innocent and not have any skills or traits of the lineage was now a criminal. Her burden struck deep down to his soul. He pointed at the leather bound diary.

"If his confession is right here then you didn't need to commit a crime," he said.

"And let the world know about us!" Meredith answered, "that could never happen and Olive was getting wise to all of it. Plus, according to that little ledger, she ordered more hits than Al Capone. It was second nature to her."

He nodded and his shoulders hunched.

"I'm sorry," Meredith said, "but I'm not keeping anything from you unlike your sister. I want us to be together."

Hal collapsed on the floor. His hole inside had become a crater. This was too much. He balled up in a fetal position, closed his eyes and cried.

"Hal, please understand," she began to shake her head and knelt beside him, "please don't."

Hal said nothing. He needed to get away. His family was

gone. The woman next to him had to go her way and he should go his. Then he let it all go and tried to forget, the deep pain, the betrayal, the family, the man. He began to transform, but ignored himself and went to a place he had always been afraid to go, one where solitude was permanent. Something to shield him from being a man.

* * *

Too many people were here. They were all familiar yet in bad ways. This is what made the outside dangerous. He stood on some boards near a building. Some cloth was draped around him, and he shed it as he pounced on top of the nearby railing. He studied the young woman. He thought her gentle but was wrong. The wetness on her face drew his attention. Something familiar inside but they were all in danger. She was in danger.

People were bad. They had been all of his life. In one way or another, bad came from it, but what he was now, this gave peace. He needed to forget and run to his safe place. He had to go, they were evil, they were unnatural.

He hissed. He had never done such a thing in his life. None of them moved toward him.

The young woman started to speak, but he wanted no part of her evil. He turned and jumped from the railing and fled to the brush. This was home. Whatever she had become needed him no more. He was never going back. Out here he would stay, lose focus, be free, and the emptiness inside him began to heal.

He took in a view of the late afternoon sky as several birds chirped overhead. This was how it should be. He concerned himself with nothing. His heart leapt at the mere thought of finally being free.

THE BULLET

BY TREVOR ABBUD

"For my worst?" Rose asked.

"Yes, of course," Luke Hart said from one knee planted in the sand.

"The worst of my worst?"

"Yes," Luke smiled, holding out the ring.

"Even when I'm mad?"

"I'll forgive you."

"Sad?"

"I'll cheer you up."

"If I'm not pretty?"

Luke shook his head. It was difficult to imagine Rose being anything but beautiful. The curls of her sable hair crashed over her shoulders and danced with the ocean breeze as Luke stared at the wisp of white hair swaying between her eyes. When he first met her, she often hid the polio streak behind her ear. Now she kept it uncoiled at the front. Her heart-shaped, cherry-red lips were pressed tight in dispute. Luke met her profound sapphire eyes highlighted by her almond skin.

How did such a big, dumb farmer-boy win the heart of such an enthralling woman? Luke thought.

Her natural beauty, curvaceous frame, confidence, and adventurous nature made her incredibly enticing.

"Yes, even if you look like my Aunt Robert."

Her lips broke into laughter. Rose swatted the air in front of Luke, then her hands shifted back to her hips and observance filled her features. Luke felt a stab of pain in his chest. It hurt how much he loved this woman.

"If I'm angry and bitter?"

"I'll make you laugh." Luke stuck his tongue out, tilted his head, crossed his eyes, and scrunched his nose.

Rose's brows pulled up. Shaking her head, her eyes glazed over. "What if I'm so angry I don't want to laugh?"

"Easy, I'll tickle you."

Rose smirked and moved her left hand to her chest. "What if I'm hurt?"

"I'll kiss it better, Rosie."

"And if I become sick? Will you love me then?" Rose stretched her left hand out and Luke grabbed it. Her narrow eyes connected with Luke's.

Luke thought of his brittle, broken mother during her last days. He was ten when the scythe of Cancer reaped her. She had been sick for a long time, but his father's love not only remained and endured but increased. "Why does pain exist?" Luke asked his father the night after his mother's funeral. They were in the living room watching a rerun of I Love Lucy, his mother's favorite show. "Well, Lukey, without pain, love can't exist. You see, love isn't that gushy stuff you see on TV or in story books. Well, it is but it ain't really. Not to say that stuff ain't nice. Hah, one day soon you'll start to like that gushy stuff." He patted Luke's head. "But the real love, the gritty kinda' love is painful. Real love is sacrifice. Real love hurts, Lukey. Remember that. To love is to hurt but the pain is just a reminder of how much we love someone."

Luke squeezed Rose's hand.

"Till death and beyond I will care for you."

"No matter what?"

Luke slipped the ring onto her slender finger. He heard the waves break along the shore and he kissed her hand. He stayed on one knee a moment longer. "Even when it hurts."

Luke Hart stood up and scooped Rose into his arms. He swayed her, peering into those arctic eyes, and kissed her nose. "No matter what."

* * *

March 13th, 2024.

Three days ago, my life ended.

It is hard to believe that it has been ten years since I proposed to my wife. And during that time my life was a blessing. But humanity was cursed.

I suppose I should have started writing this long ago. I should have kept a journal. Something that might be found a hundred years from now and (depending on if society ever returns) they could make into a movie. However, I was a cruddy student in high school.

Life is a cruel, unfair game, and one we all must play until we inevitably lose. In my thirty-eight years of life, I have found the rewards of this world shall always be overshadowed by the challenges. And yet we fight to hang on. Pain dominates. And yet we hang on. Suffering is life. And yet we hang on. My name is Luke Hart. Love and hope are all I have. And yet I hang on. The Bullet is all I have. And yet I hang on. It hurts. And yet I hang on.

There was, in fact, another pandemic. Shortly after the M-95 masks were put away and the radio ads for the vaccination were replaced with more important things like life insurance commercials and car ads, we were hit. It happened as quickly and unforeseen as the last pandemic. It happened a year after the insane tyrant up in the northern hemisphere decided that bombing its brother country to the east was a good idea. With threats of nuclear warfare sweeping the globe, our so-called leaders decided biological warfare would be a grand plan.

It was March 1st, 2023. I remembered watching the noon news while drinking my first cup of coffee. I worked nights at the Apple Pie Hill Substation for Jersey Coast Power. There were rumors of testing biological warfare in the small town of Równia, Poland. But on the first of March, the videos and images released by the press were so horrific that they could not be real. We did not live in a Netflix horror series or a Stephen King book yet here was half-human, half-beasts roaming the small villages. What must have once been men, women, and children were malformed into raging animals. The streets were littered with burning bodies. Armed soldiers in those CM-7M gas masks were strapped with automatic rifles. Tanks rumbled in the background. Smoke, fire, and carnage littered the dirt roads.

One week later the first report of this new virus was found in central Connecticut. The United States had been attacked. We sent troops in support and the enemy sent a germ here in fatal disapproval.

We were finally hit by a nuclear bomb. Not one that would explode our flesh but instead cause sanity to erupt into a confetti of chaos. It was not what I had always imagined it would be. I imagined chemical and biological warfare would be some rocket or missile zipping through the air. I pictured some greenish smog filling the streets. But the delivery mechanism was birds. Crows. Ugly, fat, black, murders of crows. How long had they already been here? That I don't know, but things got hectic, and the world quickly became anarchy. Fleas almost ended mankind's existence so why was it so difficult to believe birds could?

It was a brew of mutated rabies crows. They can carry and not get symptoms. The CDC and WHO named the zoonotic disease Therianthropic Virus. We called it The Bullet because the virus is Rhabdoviridae which means it's bullet-shaped. Yeah, real cool right? "The Bullet Virus coming to a theater near you this Fall!" Believe me, I was a fanboy of The Walking Dead and Zombieland. But it's no longer cool when you see the look of utter fear, rage, and savagery on their faces.

It also got its "cool" name because other than burning the victim, a bullet to the spinal cord is the only way to terminate the afflicted efficiently.

I've seen those mass burnings at the pits from The Walkers of Dawn, a Doomsday cult whose dictatorship rose here in the US of A shortly after world leaders declared a global collapse. The cult's vile, manipulative leader, Maddock Furorsoul, "The Root One" as his followers christened him—yeah fucking weird, I know, but fucking dangerous too. The Root One and his Walkers of Dawn are why I've earnestly worked on keeping my cellar camouflaged. Thank God for those damn weeds I always fought to cut, and Rose said how "they made us look like white trash." But if Furorsoul knew what I was hiding...

The Bullet Virus spreads not just through a bite, scratch, or saliva but is extremely contagious and airborne. The world was in utter shambles far too fast for the CDC to do research. Although, as I said, our own "people" had the same trick hidden under their sleeves.

Rabies is a disease that progresses. In most cases of rabies, one suffers a furious series of delirium, abnormal behavior, hallucinations, and insomnia. The victim will also develop hydrophobia. Consider it an act of mercy that death for the infirm subject usually occurs a few days later. All this was the same except with The Bullet the person or "thing" infected is never bedridden and along with their phobias, they become bedeviled with anthropophobia, the fear of people. Those ill became increasingly aggressive and agitated causing them to attack what they fear. It became necessary to carry around a bottle of water. I for one used my son's NERF Super Soaker XP50-AP. I still carry my pistol in my hip holster and luckily haven't had to use it. Yet. Only once did I use it at all. The Walkers of Dawn haven't sent scouts to my ranch since. Two bullets and two holes in the heads of their sick-minded pawns were warning enough, I hope. Anyway, in many cases the sick suffers from a hyper sort of dystonia where the spine and joints gnarl, twist, and limbs lengthen, deforming the ill. Some of these victims are forced to move on all fours but are fast due to accelerated hypertrophy. It's truly the most horribly remarkable thing to have happened to mankind.

The XP50 really helps.

* * *

Friday, March 13th, 2023.

One year ago. Shit got real. March along the Jersey Shore still had a nasty bite. And this March the bite was as fierce as a bullet. In under two weeks after the initial "attack" things got out of hand. "Germinating" was the popular term used by officials. The streets around town were eerie. I remember driving down Newman Square, the main strip in town. Kids on bikes and people walking their dogs were replaced by Khaki

Humvees cruising the roads. Some with big red crosses on the sides and others with armored-plated machine gun turrets and there were even some small tanks. More alarming than the tanks was the growing number of cawing crows hanging around everywhere it seemed. They destroyed the crops around my one-acre property. But at this time, I did not come across any of the inflicted that were rumored to be scattered about. Little did I know the streets would be littered with the Mads, as they've been named, in just a couple of weeks.

Only essential workers were allowed to operate. What qualified as an "essential worker" was a short, strict list. I was sent home from JCP for the remainder of that week due to potential contact with a positive employee. Fever, nausea, and inflammation in the sinuses, throat, and voice box were the initial symptoms. But it wasn't until twelve to twenty-four hours later when The Bullet really shot. Then the phantoms haunted you, and fear enveloped you. That's when you end up on the street or hiding in the woods or shot dead. Again, I hadn't seen this firsthand at this point.

They never told me who the potential contact was, but I knew it was Denis Stentz. He was one of those guys that didn't believe in personal space. Denis Stentz spat when he talked. And that Wednesday morning he was coughing along with spitting. Always spitting was Stentz. During our coffee break, I was shot with Cheez-Its shrapnel.

"It's all a hoax from The Machine, man I'm tellin' ya. They want a coup d'état. Scare the shit outta' us, then manipulate us like guinea pigs." Stentz used his forearm to cover his mouth while hacking his brains out. He had the sleeves of his coverall rolled up revealing a tattoo of a black eagle with red talons and a red beak. Probably it was a machine that did this. That, or a witch's cauldron. I thought.

I had been impressed by the thirty-three-year-old German's

French. And Denis was right. There was a coup d'état but unfortunately, it wasn't any trick by The Machine. Only a few months later when I was riding my John Deere Gator into town to look for supplies and out in front of the Scrubby Ducky Laundromat, I spotted a group of The Walkers of Dawn jump out of an old gray minivan and use a large hog catcher and taser on Denis Stentz. I knew it was Denis because I recognized the German Imperial Eagle tattoo on his arm. They would bring Denis to the Purging Pit. By midsummer, you could smell the bodies burning from miles away.

Let me retrace my steps.

Okay, so I was off work that Thursday for a four-day weekend. A weekend of playing Monopoly and Mario Kart, watching cartoons with the kiddos, eating ice cream for dinner, and after the kids were asleep, I was sipping some wine (something I rarely could do working second shift) with my wife getting tipsy and silly and watching one of her reality T.V shows. I didn't care what we watched because I was just looking forward to making a fire and snuggling up with her on the couch. Despite what we'd heard and seen on the news, Rose and I weren't worried. Little did I know I would never step foot in the substation again. Neither did I know my perfect, tiny life was about to tear me to pieces. There would be no ice cream and no SpongeBob, but plenty of fire.

Before I continue, I want to say that it was not Stentz's fault. I am immune to The Bullet Virus. But there are other bullets I am not immune from. It was my fault. I fucked up. I should have been more careful. It was dumb to take Jacob with me. Maybe the four of us could have survived together.

On Thursday morning I told Rose to sleep in, "Dad's got the little monsters this morning." By monsters, I meant my seven-year-old daughter Miley and four-year-old son Jacob. "You need the beauty sleep more than me." This was of course not true. However, I often wonder what worthy deed I must have done for a big, burly, Paul Bunyan-looking brute like me to snag such an alluring woman. I mean, I do own an ax and a peavey which I use quite often living in the pine barrens of New Jersey. I do have green eyes. But I bet it was my peavey skills.

"Oh, thank you, Mr. Hart. What time is it?" Her voice was frail and dreamy with sleep. The single stroke of white hair fell across Rose's face; the rest of her spiraling locks spilled around her tranquil features. I was standing at the bedside already dressed in what Rose called my "protagonist Fall outfit": dark blue jeans, a white undershirt, and my Grandad Jack's brown canvas jacket. I'd spice the look up with my felt Illinois-brown campaign hat handed down from my grandad. Rose called me Indiana Jones. I took it as a compliment.

"Early," I said. Children do not understand the concept of sleeping in until their teenage years.

"I shall repay you later." Her whisper was barely audible as she winked. She slept on her side in one of my T-shirts. I pinched her thigh, "I bet you will. Need my toenails clipped."

She moaned agitatedly. "Eww, leave me be." and I did after a playful pinch on her half-exposed butt cheek and a gentle kiss on her cheek.

I walked into the living room to find Miley sitting cross-legged on the couch reading a Berenstain Bears book. Miley had her dad's emerald eyes but her mom's olive skin and ebony hair and that day she wore an orange tutu and rainbow Sherbet tights and wore green and blue monster claw slippers. Adorned on her head was a lobster headband. My Miley was full of creativity and imagination. She had the sweetest soul. My son Jacob, on the other hand, had trouble keeping his clothes on. He was lying down on the floor in nothing but his Star Wars briefs playing with a Lego Minifigure and an amputee Incredible Hulk.

"Good morning, booger," I said to Miley.

"Hey!" She looked up from her book and shook a fist at me. "Good morning, nose."

"Hungry honey?"

"Can I have a playdate with Joseline?"

I bent down scooting the lobster back a touch and kissed her head. "I'll talk to Mommy, okay? Remember sickies are going 'round."

"Okay, I'm hungry for cereal."

"Okay miss, hey Rugrat, want some Cap'n Crunch?"

The one-armed Incredible Hulk crushed the Lego cowboy in half. "I want an ice pop, Daddy."

"How 'bout some Trix?"

But when we walked to the kitchen, and I looked in the fridge there was no milk.

"We have a mission."

So, Miley went back to the living room to color in her journal and Jacob and I headed into town.

"Don't wake Mommy. We're on a top-secret mission. Highly classified."

Miley gestured a thumbs up, winked, and nodded her head.

"Copy that."

John Dole, who coached me in youth football, owned Dole's Mom-and-Pop Store. It was one of the last businesses opened in our town. Most places had either switched to mobile orders only or had shut down for the indeterminate future.

Coach Dole was a tall, looming presence with hands that could cover the front page of a Sports Illustrated Magazine and fingers as thick as sausages. There seemed to be something intrinsic about his size that told you to be obedient. Coach Dole didn't have to raise his voice for you to get low and drive that dummy sled back.

Dole was in his late sixties now. His large black beard had turned to gray mustache, and his black crew cut diminished to an asymmetrical bald scalp. I stood six-three and had to look up to meet Dole's eyes.

We had put our face masks on and headed into the dimly lit store. It was one of those spots where you could get a fresh pork roll, eggs, and cheese (just don't ask Coach Dole or his wife Lacey for Taylor ham—it's an ancient Jersey quarrel—because they won't acknowledge you) and laundry detergent.

"Morning coach."

Coach Dole was behind the counter fiddling with the cash register. His camo face-covering hung around his neck.

"Say hello, Jacob."

Jacob hugged my leg and waved. Coach Dole usually had a Dum-Dum for Jacob. But today John Dole was extra quiet and fidgety. I noticed that the corners of his mouth had dried white gunk. He mumbled something then clawed, yes clawed at his scalp. For some reason, I hadn't noticed the scab-littered top of Dole's head until then.

"Coach?"

John Dole wiped his sweaty brow and whispered to himself. He inhaled deeply and I heard nasal mucus slush.

"Where's Lacey?"

Dole's eyes darted from me to Jacob and then back to the register. His mouth hung open and produced a low, strenuous hum.

"Say again, coach?"

"Below par. Got the sniffles." he managed in a harsh, gravelly, grumble.

"Hope you feel better coach. Just here for some milk, c'mon Jay."

I should have left right then and was about to sneak behind an aisle and out, but Jacob yanked on my pants leg. It was absurdly stupid of me to have gone out and especially dumb to have brought Jacob with me.

"Daddy, can you get me that?" He pointed at a plastic tactical knife toy. And because I am a six-foot-three child we got a gallon of 2% milk and a plastic knife.

Coach Dole seemed more coherent two minutes later when we checked out. He had stopped fiddling with the register. I later realized he must have been hallucinating and was trying to squish something with his finger like an ant. There was a fresh line of blood from Dole's head to his brow as he rang up the items and handed Jacob the plastic tactical knife along with a strawberry Dum-Dum.

Then he sneezed while saying goodbye.

* * *

I knew Jacob was sick that next morning and perhaps should have told Rose what happened at Dole's.

Jacob had developed a runny nose and a cough overnight but those are common for all young kids. On Friday night while Rose and I were watching an episode of Monk we heard the most disturbing scream that I have ever heard. It was painful, grating, like fangs against a chalkboard. Screaming was coming from the kitchen, on the opposite side of the ranch.

I cannot describe the pure horror that sank into my soul at the sight of my child. Jacob was in his Mickey Mouse underwear and stood with his twig legs arched like QB under center. We stopped at the entryway, and he was near the door that leads to the backyard, leaving ten feet between us.

49

He saw us and the yells became crude whimpers. It was heartbreaking to see our four-year-old in such a state. There was a thick, rubbery transparent-green discharge pouring out of both nostrils and running down his chest. Some of the mucus had dried on his chin and chest and his lips were caked with a crusty, brownish-pink substance. He stared at us through one bloodshot eye that was so inflamed and bulging from the side of its socket that it looked like an ostrich's eye. It protruded from anxiety and anger. The other eye was swollen shut and covered in a wax film that looked like a honeycomb.

"Swagger?" My fatherly instincts told me to wipe his face but instead instinctively threw my arm out grabbing Rose by the waist. He had the plastic tactical knife gripped in one bruised, enlarged fist. His other hand dangled at his side, gnarled, and had nodes growing at each knuckle. His thumb had grown a third knuckle overnight. Although his eyes were wide and filled with rage, he possessed a strange sense of self-confidence as he stood tall with his head turned up and hands stretched like talons.

"Jacob, honey Mommy's here." Rose's voice was calm but frail. "Let's get you a tissue and a warm glass of milk." She leaned forward but I held her back. "You can dip Graham Crackers."

His mouth hung slightly open, emitting a constant gurgle. It's the sound all Mads make. Like gargling salt water. It's a constant painful, irritating noise that never stops.

I despise that damn sound.

"Jay man, wanna' fruit snack?"

His knees bent and he raised the knife over his head. The muscles and veins on his neck bulged. That scared the shit out of me. Not accepting the fruit snack told me that something was very, very wrong.

"Luke, let me go to him." I put my arms down because of the terror and strain behind her words.

Rose crouched and opened her arms like so many times in the past. Every time Jacob saw those loving, welcoming arms open wide for his embrace he accepted. Inside those arms was a haven where boo-boos stopped hurting and night terrors vanished.

He growled, spraying spittle at Rose and swung the plastic knife towards us. In a remarkably quick motion, he spun on his bare heels, moved to all fours, and dashed out the doggy door I had installed for our Australian Shepherd dog, Lulu. Lulu passed away a few winters ago.

We bolted after him, but he was fast and evasive. We called the cops, and they had no luck finding him either. According to the authorities, search and rescue teams were already stationed in our county by the National Guard. It turned out Jacob was one of the first cases of The Bullet Virus in our town. I searched for him for two days without sleep. My little guy was lost. By the end of the weekend, I learned those numbers tripled.

Two days after Jacob ran away, Rose started coughing and sneezing. I was determined to not be so ignorant this time. Sunday night I came in from my search for Jacob tired and drenched by the rain. Rose was on the couch crying, tears and snot running down her face. But it was the beads of sweat slashing down the sides of her face that told me she had been shot by The Bullet Virus. She whispered something repeatedly. At first, I thought she was still in shock and agony from the loss of our son.

"Rose?"

Her glassy eyes were sad and lost as she looked up. Her expression betrayed a deep sense of longing for something that was just out of reach. And that "something" was her sanity.

"Rose?" I sat next to her. She flinched when I hugged her,

and I could feel her resisting my touch and pulling away. No! I scooted away leaving a couch cushion between us. I held back tears. I knew my Rose was stranded on a dark, lonely island where nightmares had legs. I could feel my heart break as I looked into her sullen eyes. I wanted to be her lighthouse, guiding her back home.

"Stop, stop... Mmmh. Get out, get out, get out. Mmmh." Rose twirled a strain of her black hair around her forefinger and plucked it out. "Fucking worms... drilling... my brain." She twisted another hair strand and pulled. She rocked back and forth and this time she quickly twisted and plucked three single strands consecutively. "Ow, ow, ow. Luke?"

"Yes, Rose?" I embraced her. She looked up at me and said, "I'm scared. I don't know what's happening to me."

I held her close and said, "It's okay. I'm here. I won't let anything bad happen to you."

She buried her head in my shoulder and I placed a hand on her cheek.

The touch of my hand caused her to shudder. Rose screamed, covering her ears with her hands. She tumbled forward to the floor and curled in a fetal position. "Stop it! Please stop!"

"They want to know where Jacob is. Tell them I don't know. Oh God, I promise I don't know, I don't know!"

"Mommy?" Miley asked, peeking her head into the living room. Her eyes were red from crying and her face pale. She hadn't eaten since learning about her brother.

"Get back upstairs honey."

"Mommy!" She cried.

Rose hissed and jammed a finger in both ears.

"Miley, go to your room now," I yelled.

Miley turned and I heard her footsteps stomping up the steps and then the door of her room slamming. My heart broke for my daughter. I did not feel strong enough to deal with this. How could my little girl handle it?

I turned back to my wife. "Rose?"

When I tried to help her up, she uncurled and dug her nails into my cheek. "Maggot King!"

I retreated to the kitchen and cried until I had no more tears. I checked on Rose about twenty minutes later, she was sucking her forefinger on the floor and plucking her lush raven hair. I mixed a dose of ZzzQuil into a glass of iced tea and placed it close by. She drank it immediately and crushed the glass cup with her fist.

She was asleep fifteen minutes later. I carried her to the cellar and brought blankets and the mattress from the guest room. That was the last time I held my wife.

I now understand that Jacob is what we call an Elite Mad. He lives in a world of fear and confusion, but at least I know he is still alive. It's a very strange and complicated scenario and perhaps many would rather wish death to bring peace to a loved one in a situation like this.

An Elite Mad means he is not like most Mads that roam around helplessly barking, snarling, frightened, and angry. Yes, still very vicious but controllable. These Elites are different beasts. Regular Mads are more like zombies. Elite Mads are like Werewolf zombies. Their physical transformation exceeds a Mad. It was almost three weeks later when I saw my son again. Binoculars became part of my essential tools along with the water gun and pocketknife. I was drinking my first cup of black coffee—no more luxuries like cream and sugar—while scanning the woods for Mads and Walkers of Dawn when I spotted him. He was sniffing around near an old shed about a hundred yards from our back deck. His spine had expanded along with his arms making it much more efficient for moving on all fours. He had grown about a foot and had found a pair of gray sweatpants that fit him well. Whatever horror was now haunting his mind, I'm happy he had enough awareness to clothe himself. However, his pants were inside out, and I had to resist the urge to fix them. Putting clothes on inside out was a trait of Jacob's and seeing that brought on a bittersweet wave of tears. Jacob still had the plastic tactical knife wedged in his honed teeth and that made me feel like I was with him in a way. Deep down, past his infected mind, somewhere in his soul where The Bullet hadn't wounded, he needed a part of his dad.

I set traps to catch him, and part of my fatherly side is proud he has outsmarted his old man. A year later, Jacob looks nothing like my little Swagger. He is more animal than a boy now. I try not to think about his claws, but about the toy knife he carries in his mouth. He may be drawn to the shed by human instinct still buried deep within him. After almost six months of sniffing my damn New York Giants Super Bowl XLVI varsity jacket I set out for him, he decided to force it on himself. By that time the weather was getting cooler again. To be honest it kind of fits well with his long limbs.

I hang on to the hope that maybe after enough time, the virus will run its course and he'll get better. A cold takes a few days to get over so maybe The Bullet finally dies after eighteen months?

But I doubt I'll still be alive to see it.

* * *

For over a year, Miley and I survived since Miley got her mom's looks and brains but her dad's immune system. Jacob still visited the shed. By Christmas, he had grown two feet taller, and his face was covered with chestnut fur from under his eyes and down his neck. But he had somehow cut his hair which had been down past his shoulders. Instincts I assume.

We had a few scares with Mads creeping around, but Miley followed the rules. Water pistol for the Mads, pocket-size air horn for the Elites because they weren't so afraid of water, but the loud blast scared the shit out of them, and most importantly, the taser gun for the Regs. Even with biological monsters, humans take the cake. Congratufuckinglations. Miley knew not to leave her water gun out in the cold. And the number one rule of ours was never—no matter how challenging it might be— never get too close to Mom. I guess I made that rule more for my own sake.

Rose's full, perky cheeks had sunken, the flesh of her defiant jawline pulled taunt with fear, her olive skin spoiled to a waxen hue, her smooth forehead was littered with frightened wrinkles, and bruised bags of confusion pulled down under her eyes. Rose was a spoiled fruit. She degenerated into an emaci-ated and gaunt rag of zombie's bones. To be completely honest it was difficult looking at her behind the mockup cell I had welded from metal stock I "borrowed" from Metal Works. She had ripped out all her hair save for the handful of snow-white hair I had tied in a ponytail. I did such deeds when she was sedated with Pentotropin, a very strong benzodiazepine tran-quilizer. Another rule was to only tranquilize her when neces-sary and only I could go near or enter her cell. I hated the idea of Rose being some prisoned animal in a cage. About once a month I groomed her as best as I could. I looked forward to that time and imagined she enjoyed the gentle kiss I placed on her raw, chapped lips. Miley looked forward to picking out a different lipstick shade for me to apply on her mother. But I was careful because Mads, even those not considered Elite, were very strong and unpredictable.

The Walkers of Dawn were our biggest threat. I even had a confrontation with that Hilter wannabe, Maddock Furorsoul, at Dollar Pizazz. I despise men like that. Men who prey on the weak and fearful in times of disaster and otherwise couldn't get a Golden Retriever to follow them. Maddock, the powdery face cult leader, who despite all the bright makeup and glitter looked to be in his mid-sixties. The man wore a steampunk top hat missing the cap and was bejeweled with cogs and gears. God, the phoniness bled off that theatrical cocksucker. His long, thin, gray hair was a tangled labyrinth of colorful hair clips and red and gold ribbons. His grimy black Victorian trench coat made him resemble a giant vampire bat. He and his clan of kooks roamed around town looking for Mads to bring to the Purging Pit and convert Regs—people like Miley and me into Walkers. They entered our town in their minivans and proclaimed from a megaphone, rigged on top of Furorsoul's vintage 1990's Chrysler Town and Country gray minivan with wood panel doors, came The Walkers of Dawn creed.

With the cleansing rains, brings the death of the sun
    Here, the killing days
    In the new dusk of mankind
    Eternal darkness they find
    Toxic blood flows, fear the drought
    Man's ignorance
    The Purge
    Day of the Dead, will be our last bout
    Cast into the reaping pool, we pray to the Moon of blood
    The dawn's surge
    The demons, we promise to severance
    This be our penance

I was grabbing some soap, napkins, and coloring books for Miley when I bumped into "The Root One" in the middle of an aisle. I was surprised he allowed himself to be separate from his lunatic lynch mob. I was face to face staring into the blue lens of his bronze steampunk goggles. The goggles had two-inch spikes protruding from the frames and attached to the lens were multiple smaller lenses. They made him look like some cyber mad scientist or a cyber-insect is more appropriate. He had a gold cane in one hand and an 18-inch machete in the other.

"Well, well, well. What do we have here?" He took a step back and tossed the cane and machete to the other hand in one motion. Without his gang of loonies nearby, his pretentious charade reeked of cowardliness.

I did not say a word. I was too angry and disgusted to speak. This man sent his hounds to my home, looking to see if I was hiding any of those inflicted. This man would not think twice about capturing my Jacob with his hog catcher and taser and throwing my boy into that damn Purging Pit. I could picture him on top of some giant hill of burned corpses overlooking his damn death pit with arms raised victoriously and laughing like a fucking goblin.

My .44 Remington Magnum was pressed against his deep cleft chin without hesitation. He must have known I had shot and killed two of his minions.

"Nay, nay, I say," said Furorsoul.

I hated the way his crimson lips pinched and puckered, pinched, and puckered. He backed away and raised the machete and cane over his head. "I pray, the bringing of Dawn ignites your soul with fire." His eyes grew wide and Furorsoul spun around doing a short, stupid leap, and clicked his heels before turning towards the exit. But his circus face reappeared from around the corner. "The Bullet bites those who conspire."

A few moments later the powdered face was gone, and I thought what a stupid, stupid rhyme.

* * *

If it weren't for Miley, I would have never made it this far. I was humbled and rejuvenated by her steadfast resilience and positivity. I was astounded by my daughter's courage in the face of The Bullet. For me, the challenge of physical survival was not an issue, but mental hardship was the real monster.

So let me end this here for I am almost certainly done writing. I've told my tale and will leave you with this snare of life and the perverse, moral dilemma it poses. If anything, let this story serve as a reminder of the complexity and ambiguity of life, and how difficult it can be to make decisions guided by moral principles.

There was an accident. It's been three days and I've spent most of my time crying and vomiting.

As the sun began to rise, I enjoyed my morning coffee in my Fred Flintstone-shaped mug. I was sitting in my rocking chair on the back porch and observing the tree line with my binoculars. This had become my morning routine before checking on Rose, making breakfast, and waking Miley. It was the first day that promised hope for Spring weather. The sun was already stretching its rays and birds gossiped. I remember putting the binoculars down, standing up, and looking up at the clear sky. Inhaling deeply, I focused on my breath and savored it. The sky and the chattering birds spoke to me of hope. God, was it better than the frequent cawing of the bullying crows? I thought I heard a cry. I brought the binoculars back to my face. Was it Jacob? If it was, I'd run upstairs and wake Miley. She had yet to see her brother during the handful of times he had returned. Miley might be uncomfortable seeing

Jacob as a feral zombie, but I know she would still want to see him.

When I heard the horrible scream again, it didn't stop. In my stupid, hopeful state I aimed the binoculars toward the old shed and realized the cries were coming from around the house. Again, I thought of Jacob. Had primal instincts led him to his mother? Why had I never thought of this possibility? As if a cube of cheese was enticing a mouse before its neck got snapped by a trap, my mind was deceived by my wish!

The cellar! I spiked Fred's face on the wood decking. "No, God, please no!" I bolted towards the porch gate and used both hands to vault over it. The screaming increased for a short moment, then faded, and by the time I reached the cellar door there was silence. That silence was the most awful sound I ever heard.

Before I write down this final part, I ask that you put yourself in my situation. I am not a doomsayer; I am an advocate for hope. If not, I wouldn't have written this. However, I am aware The Bullet will always be here.

I cannot fully explain what happened when I walked into the cellar. I heard Miley's last whimper. Her head had been severed while her tiny lips made one last useless plea. But it was clear to me that when the wailing ceased it was over. And I'm not sure which was worse, seeing my poor baby girl ripped to shreds, literally fucking shreds, or Rose crouched in the corner of her cell, picking her nose and rambling random letters. Luckily for me, she was having a bad hallucination. And all the while that damn gurgling coming from her throat. In what God-forsaken Hell had I been sent to, where a mother could do such a thing to her daughter? Suddenly, I felt my body shaking and freezing, and I barely had the strength to pull the string on the overhead light. I think we all have had that weird sensation when afraid or upset. It's like a physical numbing needle injected into our veins. Well, this was ten times worse. It sliced down my spine to my groin and thighs.

The cellar was dank, but I smelled something else immediately. Miley's blood was splattered from the ceiling to the three steps of the cellar about fifteen feet from the prison cell. Her body was sprawled against the half-opened cell door and her decapitated head had fallen upside-down. In the dim light, one lifeless eye stared at me, and the other hung from the optic nerve. Miley's dismembered left arm lay next to the spilled apple juice and bran muffin. The pink construction paper flower was soaked in apple juice and blood. Scattered on the floor were the beads from the broken necklace Miley had made Rose. The room spun and became hot. With all my strength, I crawled forward on my belly crying.

A sickening wave of heat hit my face, and something lodged in my throat. There was a feeling of drowning in the dense air. Seeing her mother in such a horrible condition had become increasingly difficult and more challenging for Miley. And she kept mentioning that she wanted to do something special for her mother's birthday next week. The only thing I did was become increasingly adamant that Miley did not get near her mother. I crawled to the cell door. Miley's purple-footed pajamas were saturated with blood. But maybe I could fix her. I was her father, and it was my job to protect her.

When I was just a few feet away my gaze paused at Miley's feet. They were the only things unharmed. Her feet were so small and cute in those footed pajamas. The first of many memories of Miley hit me. But what finally snapped me out of my painful, dazed state was the stark reality that Miley was now just a memory. I sprung to my feet thinking of wiggling Miley's precious little toes... and this little piggy went all the way home.

I stomped into Rose's cage stepping over my mauled daughter. Rage, sadness, and regret boiled in my blood. Rose, who was still picking her nose and gargling spittle, jerked up on her haunches and hissed. As she sniffed the air and growled her face pointed upwards. She positioned herself like a defensive tackle in a three-point stance.

"You fucking animal," I screamed, closing the gap between us.

Her once heart-shaped lips were now chapped and broken. They stretched in a snarl. Thick foam bubbled from her mouth. The gargling increased and her barking sounded like a revving dirt bike. My newly developed instinct rushed to my right hip and before Rose could lurch forward, I already had the XP50 pumped and aimed. I pulled the trigger, splashing her face with cold water. There was once an uncherished time when Rose would have laughed at this. But my Rose was mad and retreated against the cellar wall swatting at the water.

I moved closer now a yard away from my wife, whose hands were erect in front of her showing her claws. In another instinctive motion, the water gun was back in the makeshift holster and the .44 was in my hand.

"How could you?"

For my worse?...

"You killed our daughter, Rose!"

The worst of my worst?...

I spat at her. "Rose? Rosie... how could you... do this to our girl?" I cried.

Even if I'm mad?...

I raised the gun and pointed it at her. Rose's gargles were small and fretful.

Sad?...

I clicked the hammer back. Her dark and dingy face was speckled in freckles of Miley's blood.

If I'm not pretty?...

"Rose? Please! Please, please? Look at me." I pleaded. But she would not make eye contact with me. I begged God to just let her look into my eyes for a second, just for a second to embrace my stare, but her barbaric blue eyes darted left, right, up, and down. Then her eyes danced. She was lost and savage like a wild animal, incapable of making even a shadow of a social connection.

"Rose, look what you did to our little girl. Look what you did you goddam fucking animal. You ruined everything. Everything could have been fine. Why?" I kicked dust in her face causing her to swing her hands and bare her yellow teeth. "Our little girl... Oh, God." I puked clear stomach acid having already barfed anything else. Bent over, hands on my knees and in the far back corners of my mind hoping Rose would attack me while my guard was down. I wanted her to give me an excuse to kill her and take this moral crisis out of my hands. Let Rose and I fight to the death. With my brow furrowed, I glared at Rose. "I hate you. You are not my Rose. You will never be my Rose." I said in a low hoarse voice. Then I retched, retched, retched, and retched again falling to one knee. It felt like my stomach had been drop-kicked and my throat wrung dry. My mind was still in a mental whirlwind, and I suddenly jammed the gun barrel in my mouth. My eyes shot wide open and with all the pain and rage I gave a truly gruesome yell.

And if I become sick? Will you care for me?...

Rose jumped up, her fingers impossibly stretched and spread into weapons and her arms cocked back. The Bullet had given her a severely hunched back. Her tongue vibrated like a snake as she gave another gurgling shrill.

I stood tall too and pointed the .44 at her. I stared into her eyes. I could shoot if I just focused on those lost, maniacal eyes.

"Rose, can you hear me?"

She swung at me snorting gutturally. The white length of

hair was pasted between her eyes with a few loose threads spread over her face like long spider legs. I stared into her eyes searching for remnants of my wife. I found a stranger intruding. I pulled the trigger. Rose shrieked as gray dust blew up around her from the cement floor. I saw her shrink back but the sound made her angry. When the dust cleared, I saw her mouth and eyes wide open. "Gaaaaaar!"

I clicked the hammer back.

"You killed my daughter." A small sensation of relief came over me. It will all be over soon, I mused. Rose sprung forward and clawed at me, missing by a few feet. I instinctively snatched the XP-50 and squirted her shirt. She writhed and yelped like a rabid animal. But as I holstered the Super Soaker and directed the .44 once more, I could not summon compassion. I thought of Miley in her dinosaur costume trick-or-treating. I remembered Miley teaching me how to hula-hoop and sneaking candy into the movie theater inside her cheeseburger pocketbook. I thought of the treehouse we were going to build this summer. I thought of Jacob snuggling up in front of the fireplace the winter before The Bullet. How I missed watching Jacob feed the ducks in our pond. I thought about how I would never share a beer with my son. I thought of how he would spend the rest of his nights alone. Finally, I thought of never growing old with Rose, and all the memories we'd never get to make. I thought of all the moments The Bullet had taken away from us. I thought of all the pain and sorrow that had been inflicted upon us.

"I'm going to kill you now. You sick, sick thing."

No matter what?...

"Rose, if you're there somewhere, I love you." Our eyes locked.

... real love hurts...

Then it happened. Behind the dark clouds of Rose's primitive glare, I caught a silver lining of recognition. In a glorious fragment of a second a shred of a memory swept across her glassy gaze. In that instant, her jowls relaxed, and she knew me. A whimper escaped her trembling lips. She loved me and longed so dearly for my help and embrace I could read it in her desperate and confused eyes. I swear I saw it. A glistening twinkle reflected off her diamond eyes. My hand dropped.

"Rosie?"

The savage fire returned to her face. The whimper mutated into grunting like a demon possessed swine. And my God, was there a part of me that thought Rose still looked beautiful? Love is blind and will kick you where it hurts.

I backed away, turning, and jumping over my ruined daughter. I locked the cell door and ran back into the house, into the shower. I wept while cold water mixed with tears, along with my sanity, washed down the drain.

Hours later, I fought against my lack of courage to get Miley. And I wonder what curse had I been given to witness my wife sniffing the blood from her daughter's fucking severed head?

I buried Miley yesterday next to our dog Lulu under the twenty-foot pine tree we decorated for Christmas each year. If I'm still around next Christmas, I'll light up the tree extra special for Miley.

Rose has not returned that silver-lining gaze. There is a lackluster sparkle to her diamond eyes which do not refract but absorb light. Will one day I believe it was all in my mind? Perhaps. But for now, I know I saw it and hold onto that. I saw her see my emeralds in her diamonds just like the night I got down on one knee.

So, what will I do now? Well, there will always be The Bullet. And The Bullet comes in many forms. And when it comes to me, I will join Miley somewhere pleasant in the sun and under the shade of a big tree. But for now, I will visit Miley each morning. I will hang on. I will wait for Jacob each month. I will hang on. Maybe one day Rose will return and stay. Maybe one day Jacob will return for good. And for now, I will take care of Rose even when it hurts, till death and beyond.

No matter what.

Real love hurts.

COYOTE

BY BENJAMIN B. WHITE

T he nursing assistant – the name tag on her smock said, "Lori" – adjusted the blood pressure armband around the boy's bicep.

"Oh, my god. You have beautiful eyes," she said, letting her genuine reaction surface and escape into the hospital room, momentarily chasing her professional demeanor out.

The boy smiled.

"I'm sorry," she said. "I didn't mean to embarrass you. Are those contacts?"

"No," he replied, gazing at her so she could fully appreciate his left eye – a crystal blue – and his right eye – an ice-glistened green.

"I've heard of it, but you are the first person I've ever actually met with two different colored eyes."

He nodded. "It's the direct result of a gene pool competing for dominance."

"They are beautiful," Lori complimented as she turned the BP machine on.

The boy felt the armband tightening. "Compliment my

parents," he told her. "You should see my mother's eyes. She's Black, but her eyes are green – and brighter than mine."

"And the blue?" Lori asked as she jotted down the numbers.

"My dad's white, so his blue eyes aren't so unusual. On any given day he'll say his eyes are bluer than Paul Newman's, Frank Sinatra's, or Bob Dylan's. I don't even know who those guys are," the boy explained.

Lori smiled, looking into his eyes for signs of dilated pupils. "How do you feel?"

"I'm fine."

"No headache?"

"Oh, no. I'm okay. It was just a good hit on the football field. I was a little dizzy at first, but not bad," the boy said.

"Okay, Wally," Lori said, looking at the chart. "Oh. That's cool too. Your name, I mean. Wally Walters."

"Yeah. Everybody just calls me C'yote, or Ky, for short," he replied.

"That's terrible," she said, again letting her genuine reaction emerge into the room unfiltered.

"Wally was taken aback for a second, but then realized why she had reacted that way. "Oh, no, it's not because I am biracial."

Lori leaned closer with her head tilted slightly with empathy.

"It's because," Wally/Ky continued, "ever since I was little, I had a great skill of finding things. Like if we lost a baseball in the neighbor's garden, I could find it. Or if I couldn't find it, I could find the money we needed to go buy another one. So my friends said I was like a scavenger, and then over time, they started calling me C'yote."

"That's a great story," Lori said before a nurse knocked on the door and slowly stuck her head into the room.

"Are you okay, Lori?" The nurse asked.

"Yes," Lori replied. "I just got the vitals."

"Any sign of concussion?"

"No. Everything seems normal," Lori said. "On the surface, anyway," she added, catching herself for over-diagnosing – or wrongly diagnosing.

"Okay. The doctor will be in in a few minutes. Stay with your patient. I am going up to the furth floor. There's something going on in the pharmacy."

"What is it?"

"I don't know. I think Javier has been hurt. But stay here."

"Yes, ma'am," she said, deferring to the experience of the nurse. Lori had only been out of her two-year nursing assistant program for a couple of months and was still learning the full scope of the job.

The nurse shut the door and hurried away to the commotion on the fourth floor. It wasn't unusual for unruly patients to initiate arguments at the pharmacy, but tonight it sounded like there was more conflict with an addict demanding drugs and even going so far as to hurt one of the resident nurses, Javier. The nurse would find out what was going on, and left Lori with Ky to keep an eye on any concussion-related symptoms.

It had been a good, clean hit, but Ky wasn't sure if it had been a shoulder pad to his helmet or if his helmet hit the artificial turf. Either way, it had knocked him dizzy and raised enough concerns for the coaches and the trainer to pull him out of practice and send him in for observations.

That was definitely not the way he had wanted his high school senior football season to begin, but he was raised to be respectful and didn't push back much more than a couple of I'm-fine-Coach explanations. And besides, he reasoned, at least it was a preseason practice, and he was convinced he could feel any damage done had already healed inside his head.

Torn between two worlds
    And other worlds within those
    No wonder we howl

"We just want to keep him overnight," the doctor was saying to Mr. and Mrs. Walters who had arrived simultaneously at the hospital to see their son.

"But he's okay?" Mrs. Walters asked.

"Everything checked out. No symptoms. No accelerated heart rate. No confusion. No memory loss. And his memory – short and long term – seems to be intact."

"That's good," Mr. Walters commented. "Any headache, Ky?"

"No, sir," Ky replied, shaking his head. "I think I can go home."

"Easy," the doctor started. "Brain injuries are nothing to fool around with or take too lightly. They can have long-term effects, and sometimes the symptoms are delayed."

"I'm alright, Dad," Ky said, looking into his father's bright blue eyes. They shared a certain understanding, and Mr. Walters understood that his son's metabolism had reacted to the hit and had prevented any further damage – had in fact eradicated any damage already.

"Just as a precaution, Ky," Mrs. Walters interjected, mentally tapping into their shared bond with a sense of her own understanding. "Just one night, Doctor?"

"Just one night to stay on the safe side."

Coyote has mixed
    Bloodlines pumping history
    To transform each day

The hospital was silent, and Ky was dozing, lightly passing in and out of a dream state, when he felt a familiar presence in the room. He opened his eyes.

His eyes focused and he felt the weight of two large front paws of a canine resting on the bed. The glow of light off the monitors and out from behind the cracked bathroom door, he saw the snout of a wolf stretching its fur back to bare its teeth. Then he heard a deep, low growl as the snout – followed by the rest of the head and upright, pointed ears – moved closer, sniffing.

Blood dripped from the front fangs before being swiped away hungrily by a quick flick of an old tongue with its pinkened youth long gone and whitened by age. The breath was warm and close enough for Ky to smell fresh kill.

"What are you doing here?" A voice, slow and raspy, came forced out of the snarling face of the wolf.

"Hell, Grandfather," Ky replied, staring into the crystal blue eyes of his lineage.

"You don't need to be here," the old wolf said. Then the snout retracted, the paws lifted from the bed, and, seconds later, Ky was in the company of an old – yet well-toned – man with gray hair, strong arms, muscular legs, and a stout chest. The man looked around and went over to a closet taking a hospital gown off a shelf. He slipped it on without bothering to even attempt to tie the strings in the back.

"It's a precaution," Ky explained.

"Get up. Let's go for a hunt."

Ky smiled and shook his head slightly.

"Oh," his grandfather started, "I see. You're under your mother's let's-get-along-with-humans influence. That's why you are here."

Ky's smile broadened.

"Well, it's too bad," his grandfather softly replied to the

grandson's smile. "Chago is angry and the night will be full of retribution."

Just the mention of the name of the leader of The Righteous Group (TRG) made Ky's heart beat with excitement, and it tore him into halves split between his bicultural desires. He would love to run with his grandfather on a hunt for humans. Yet, his mother's ideologies of co-existence were equally strong within him. He loved his family – on both sides – but he knew if his father had deferred to her wishes, it was best for him to follow suit and listen to his mother and her ideas.

"It's okay," his grandfather said, recognizing the look on Ky's face and knowing the boy's decision was made. "We'll run again."

"Yes, sir," Ky replied. "Be careful."

His grandfather was at the door of the room. He had cracked it open so he could glance up and down the empty corridor. He shook the hospital gown off and tossed it in the floor beside Ky's bed. "Get well," he said facetiously – knowing any injury his grandson may have had was cured instantly after it had happened.

"Thank you," Ky said.

The old man quickly transformed back into a wolf. Ky could hear his large padded paws disappearing into the silence of the hospital.

Grandfather werewolf
   Haunted by transformations
   Fear runs through blood

"Are you catnapping?" The night nurse asked, making her rounds and noticing Ky's eyes were open.

He thought about how totally wrong "catnapping" was, but smiled and said, "Yes. I'm in and out. Just dozing."

"Any headache? Or blurred vision?"

"Oh, no. I'm fine," Ky replied.

"That's good," the nurse said, but then she grinned – a grin that made Ky think he was in a shallow dream state that was eerily complicated by the nurse suddenly transforming into another human.

Ky had to be dreaming, yet he still heard his own voice ask, "Eddie?"

"Who were you expecting, the night nurse?"

"Well, yeah," Ky responded.

The nurse-turned-Eddie laughed.

Ky tried to wake up, but all he could manage was, "Man, I've got to wake up," wondering why he was dreaming of Eddie – the guy who worked at the café with the pastry chef. What's her name? Luna.

"You aren't dreaming, Ky," Eddie said, interrupting the train of thought.

"It would make more sense if I was dreaming," Ky replied.

"Not when you hear my message." Eddie shook his head slightly.

"Message?"

"Yes, It's from Chago."

"Chago? What does ... How does he even know me?"

"He knows your family, and he is recruiting ... no. He is actually activating packs for a push against human arrogance."

"What?"

He knows your grandfather and he wants you to join the push."

"Wait – what?" Does he know my whole family?" Ky asked.

"He knows your bloodline is mixed, But he wants you to follow your father's natural heritage and fight against humans."

Ky was silent.

Eddie continued, "But I have delivered the message, so think it through. But remember Chago is not one to be ... disappointed."

"But, Eddie, why are you delivering the message – you're not even a ... what are you?"

"I am a transhuman – able to take on the exact shape and mind of any other human – dead or alive – or even unborn."

Ky had never heard of a transhuman. "But, why ..."

"I follow Chago," Eddie explained. "I work for Chago."

"Like a minion?" Ky responded with no small amount of disrespect – a sudden urge of disgust.

"I like 'familiar' better," Eddie answered, unfazed.

Ky stared at him.

"Anyway," Eddie broke the silence, "think about it and take my advice – join the activation." Then Eddie closed his eyes, turned around 360 degree, and suddenly reappeared as the night nurse. She turned away from Ky and walked out the door.

A few seconds later, the door reopened and the night nurse looked into Ky's room.

"I got the message. Just go!" Ky said.

"I'm just checking on you, Wally." Are you okay?" The night nurse said.

"Oh. I'm sorry. A dream. I'm fine. Thank you."

Animalistic
    Love and lust go hand in hand
    The heart is a beast

The rest of Ky's night was full of anxiety and thoughts of Chago's plans to carry out a "push" against humans; an "activation." But Ky knew those words were code for war.

His father had warned him there would come a time for him to make a choice between his bloodlines. Ky was the offspring of two distinct channels of lycanthrope ideologies – "the two camps" his father had called it. One based on the concept of being equal to and partners with humans; the other based on the desire to break out against the dominance of humans and the arrogance of their species. Ky was raised to operate in the human world while keeping his true identity separate – and secret.

Lori, the nursing assistant, came into Ky's room the next morning. "How are you feeling?" She asked.

Ky caught himself staring a little too hard to make sure she was really Lori, then said, "I'm good. How are you?"

"Great, thank you. I was hoping they hadn't discharged those beautiful eyes yet," she said, obviously flirting.

"Well, if they had, I'd be sitting here blind, unable to see you," he flirted back, hoping his humor didn't come across as stupidity.

She smiled, pretending to straighten up the room and picking up the hospital gown, wondering to herself why it was on the floor. Then she said, "I want to ask you something."

She looked around the room cautiously. Ky was intrigued. He would have sworn he saw a passing hint of her mouth and lower jaw elongating, then quickly retracting.

"Do you know Birger? Or the websites he posts?"

Ky tilted his head and looked at her, then smiled. "I don't know him. But I do know of him."

"Last night, I saw your family mentioned on one of his posts."

"Really," Ky said. Now he was the one being cautious.

Lori reached up with both hands and took a designer contact out of her eye. As she looked back up, Ky saw that the eye – that had been gray – was now the natural crystal green of her naked eye.

"I don't like to draw attention to myself," she explained, "not working around these ... my colleagues."

"I understand," Ky said, nodding his head.

"And," Lori continued as she put her gray-tinted contact back in her eye, "I usually don't hit on the patients, but would you like to go to lunch with me? I get off at noon."

"Will I be discharged by then?" Ky asked.

"You are about to be discharged as soon as the doctor sees you one last time."

"Should I wait for you?"

"No need. Just meet me at the pastry café. They have great sandwiches."

"Okay."

"My friend Luna works there as well. Though maybe not today. Her boyfriend was hurt last night. Here in the hospital, actually."

"Oh?"

"Yeah. But he'll be fine."

"That's good," Ky said.

Lori nodded. "Luna has a great skill of recognizing exactly what kind of pastry customers want."

"I think I know her. Eddie works with her."

"You know Eddie?" She asked.

"A little. Just from the café."

"Then I won't hurt your feelings if I tell you to avoid him."

Ky chuckled in agreement. "Not at all."

"Good. He hangs out with ..." she hesitated, "... disruptive forces."

Ky felt a sudden wave of affection for Lori. He nodded –

understanding – and his mind was persuaded that his future leaned toward her. "What's your favorite pastry?" He changed the subject.

"I like the lemon scones. Weird, I know. And I am guessing you like something more along the lines of caramel pecan Danishes."

"Maybe Luna's not the only one with that superpower."

There are all kinds of
    Power to be discovered
    Her soft smile sparkled.

GREY WOLF

BY PATRICK SCOTT

Standing on the subway platform, Rog noted the two younger men gesturing to the older woman coming down the stairs into the station. He released a familiar low sigh. He told himself his time was tight, so he could not get caught up in anything else tonight. He pulled the coat he wore when working tighter around his lean frame.

He turned back toward the terminal where the sound of the oncoming train pricked at his ears. Rog checked for the space between everyone. With his deep brown eyes, he glanced down the track seeing the woman, her hair cut short and still shaggy in the fashion of the day, arrive about even with him one and half car lengths to his left. He picked up an odd scrape from one of her pursuer's footsteps. Rog guessed one of them had a limp from an old altercation.

"Hey there," a high reedy voice said barely above a whisper. "Where you going?"

Even without turning, Rog smiled a crooked smile. He had a picture in his mind of the one who spoke. He lowered his head as though checking to make sure his shoes were tied. Rog used his peripheral vision to see the talker on the woman's far side. He nodded in self-satisfaction having called it.

Rog suspected the talker presented a specific kind of trouble. He knew the threat from Talker was not physical in origin, but much more dangerous since he thought of himself as the brains of the outfit comporting himself accordingly. If he intervened, Rog was not going to have to attack him first.

Rog was far more worried about the damage the bulky man resembling a shambling former lineman could do. Fortunately, he gauged by the way the bigger man stood that he was the one with the hurt leg.

"Hey," Talker said again. "I asked you something."

"Oh, I thought you were talking to someone else."

Despite the direct answer, Rog heard the slightest quaver and guessed she came into the city for the night getting hung up at dinner. He gave her a quick once over too. Rog figured her to be a nice librarian or maybe a bookkeeper. He equated her fastidious dress and stature to that of someone used to being in a much more controlled environment.

"No, I was talking to you. Where are you from?"

Rog could not resist shaking his head. He heard things like this more frequently than he cared to admit. He saw it having the desired result driving the others, who were scared of the confrontation, farther back and isolating the men and the librarian. He started thinking of her simply as the role he assigned to her.

"I'm just heading home," the librarian said.

"That's not what I asked you," Talker said. "You hear that Hulk? She's offering to have us come over."

The big lineman, apparently named Hulk, grunted. Without moving an inch closer, he seemed to menace the woman further. The big man stayed quiet letting Talker do what he did best.

"No," Librarian said a little sharply. "I wasn't doing that. You ...." She seemed to be looking for the best words to describe the two men. "Gentlemen need to leave me alone."

Rog noticed her hand going into her purse at her hip while the strap bisected her chest. He could see her gripping her keys like claws or grabbing her canister of pepper spray she got at one of her girlfriend's self-defense courses. Noting the confined space and the likely affect of it, he shook his head slowly noting the confined space and the likely effect of aerosolized cayenne or ghost peppers.

Slipping his shoulders down, Rog turned slowly to face the odd trio. He took two soundless steps until he stood practically behind Hulk.

"Guys," he said softly. "Why don't you head home?"

He did his best to suppress the smile playing at the corners of his lips at the jump by Hulk. Rog found silence to be an excellent tool for catching those who are unsuspecting off guard.

Talker recovered first as was normal in this situation. "What are you talking about? We're just having a conversation with the lady. Why don't you just step off?"

Rog noted the nervous staccato. He guessed these two were used to much less resistance in their victims. He presented a problem for them. Rog found little to care about in that regard.

"Is that true?" Rog asked the librarian.

He waited for the expected body reposition of Hulk between him and their quarry. He saw the limp in the left leg. Rog guessed it was the knee.

"Of course, it is," Talker shot back.

"Why don't you let the lady answer since I was asking her?"

Rog leaned out a fraction and met the woman's eyes. He noticed how striking her eyes were. He had never seen eyes the palest shade of blue causing them to look like an overcast sky. He tried to reassure her with a simple look. Rog could not tell if it was working.

"Is that true, Ma'am?" he asked.

"These men are-"

He lost the next few words as Hulk's meat paw came up meeting the side of his head. Rog saw a slight burst in his left eye. He stumbled close to the lip of the trench. He caught himself.

He looked up at the woman first. Rog was struck by how impassive her face appeared. He then saw the stony resolution in Hulk's expression and the bright excitement in Talker's. He straightened up.

"Boys, I'm giving you a chance here," Rog said meeting both their gazes. "I know you think you know what's going to happen, but you don't. This is your one chance and I urge you, strongly, to take it."

"Shit," Talker said in his high squeak. "There're two of us and one of you. You wouldn't be able to handle Hulk all by yourself."

Rog straightened up. "Your friend is a big one for sure and I have no doubt that he's used to getting his way with the most minimal amount of effort." Rog met Hulk's eyes directly gauging the overconfidence in his positioning and face. "You don't want to do this."

When Hulk predictably lunged for him, Rog slid to one side and drove a fist into his left knee. He felt pain shoot up his hand as though he had struck a solid piece of forged steel. Rog did his best to keep the supernaturally painful grimace from showing on his face. He swallowed back the fury and excruciating pain.

Hulk grinned as though completely expecting the action by Rog. The bulkier man closed his hand into a ham sized fist.

Hulk brought the fist down with incredible force. He laughed in the back of his throat as though hearing a joke for the first time.

"Hey," Rog croaked. "Cut that out."

Watching the fist rise again before interlacing with the other hand for a doubly painful blow, Rog rammed his fist into the opposing knee. He heard the satisfying crack. Rog wondered if he had broken Hulk's knee. He saw the man wobble. Rog drove a second blow into Hulk's crotch.

Rog backed up in time to see Hulk fall and curl up into a fetal position while writhing on the floor of the station in pain. He checked to make sure there was no more fight left in Hulk.

Rog rose from the ground. Turning back to Talker and Librarian, he shook his head at what he saw. He instantly spied the knife held in a shaky hand up to Librarian's porcelain neck. Rog checked her still eyes for any sign of concern. He found nothing remotely akin to terror resting there. He started growing concerned.

"Put the knife down," he growled.

The train came up behind him. The loud whoosh of wind entered with the vehicle. The doors on the train open with a distinctive sliding sound.

Rog swallowed back the urge to violently attack Talker, breaking him into a million little pieces. He watched Talker dragging Librarian closer to the train. He spared a quick glance to Hulk, who remained on the ground.

"Wait, let her go," he commanded.

"Naw," Talker sneered. "I don't think you'll stop me. Especially, since I've got this nice lady with me and you don't want to hurt her."

As Rog prepared to answer with his fists, he felt something tug slightly at his pants leg. He looked to see Hulk reaching for him to grab hold. Rog was unsure if the move sought to do him harm or merely give Talker an opening to get away with their prey. Rog kicked the bigger man in the head. He watched the light leave Hulk's eyes as unconsciousness claimed him.

Rog turned in time to see Talker forcing Librarian onto the train. He cursed himself for getting distracted. Reaching forward, Rog felt the door slam closed at his wrist. He pressed his arm deeper into the train car hoping to put his hand on Talker who continued backing away from the door.

He saw the train start moving. Rog took a few steps to keep up. He picked up the pace seeing the wall fast approaching. At the last minute, Rog yanked his arm out growling in frustration.

He felt a strong urge to save the Librarian. Rog decided to get a little help. He pulled out his phone and started for the stairs.

"Baker," the voice at the end of the call said. "Go."

"Hey," Rog said.

"Oh, damn," Baker said in a strained tone. "What the hell did you do now?"

"I was helping."

"I doubt that very seriously."

Rog headed for the stairs. "I don't care whether you believe me or not. I need you to stop the 312 southbound. If you can do it before it reaches the next station, that would be great."

"Why am I doing such a thing?" Baker asked. "Because you know it will likely be my ass no matter what. I just want to make sure that I'm getting chewed out for something good."

"You are." Rog exited the station and broke into a run hearing Baker clicking through a series of commands on his keyboard. "For one, you have a particularly bad guy named Hulk currently resting his eyes on the platform. You're going to want to send someone to pick him up."

"For what?"

"He was complicit in harassing a woman on the platform

with his partner who got her on the train." Rog dodged a few people and saw the next station's sign a few blocks down. "Any luck stopping it or are you going to make me run all the way to Lex?"

"I'm working on it," Baker snapped. "So he was just menacing someone. You know unless she presses charges that's never going to stick."

"He hit me and you know I'll be in court for you."

"It doesn't sound like you're too worse for wear," Baker joked. "In fact, I would say you're doing better than usual if you're running."

"It's because he's got a woman," Rog said between breaths. "Now, stop the damn train. I'm going down. Will it be there?"

"It'll be there," Baker said. "I'm sending you back up too. Don't do anything stupid."

"You mean aside from running after a guy with a knife?" Rog asked.

"You didn't tell me he was armed."

Rog bounded down the stairs two at a time. "You're not worried for me, are you?"

He scanned for the southbound line. Spying the spot, he sprinted for it heading down those stairs with the phone still pressed to his ear. He saw a platform full of people waiting for the train, but the space remained empty.

"Baker," he shouted into his phone. "Where's the train? Did you not stop it in time?"

"I did just what you asked," Baker said with a note of exasperation. "I stopped the train before it got to the station."

Rog sprinted for the tunnel coming to a halt at the edge of the platform. "Are you in communication with the engineer?"

"I am. He's screaming at me about making him late and this affecting his performance evaluation." Baker laughed. "I told him there was something bigger than his quarterly bonus going on, but he snapped back something about his wife already spending the money."

"Ask him if he sees a skinny guy with long lanky black hair in a too big leather jacket."

Rog waited impatiently for a reply from Baker. Looking around the platform, he found most of the people pulled back from him. Rog needed none of them getting in his way.

"He sees him," Baker said.

"Holding a knife and clutching a woman a shade shorter than him with blondish brown hair?"

Rog struggled to recall the woman's hair color, but he found he could only think about her eyes. Rog consoled himself with the fact Talker likely had not changed victims once he got in the train.

"Though he's starting to get a little twitchy," Baker said. "He probably knows something is up at this point."

"Making him a lot more dangerous," Rog said. "How precise can you be starting and stopping getting the train in here?"

"Pretty precise. Why?"

"I want to see if you can move it up enough to get the first set of passenger doors right inside the station. If you do that, I might be able to get him."

"Are going to rush him?" Baker asked.

"Hopefully, I won't have to," Rog answered. "Just get it to the platform and I'll do the rest."

"Love that confidence. You ready?"

"Count to twenty and the roll them in here. And tell the engineer not to do anything.". Rog lowered into a squat at the edge of the tunnel and low enough not to be seen through the windows. "I don't need him mucking things up."

"Alright," Baker said. "Good luck, Rog. Make sure you don't get killed. I don't want to have to fill out any paperwork."

As way of response, Rog ended the call without saying a word. He stuffed the phone into his back pocket. He opened and closed his mouth several times before hanging his jaw wide and popping it. His muscles flexed in a graceful wave.

He heard the subway roll and pressed his body to the wall. Out of concern, Rog threw a quick look over his shoulder. He saw most of the patrons had backed up farther. He noted the promised back up had not arrived yet. Rog felt relief at not needing to coordinate with any of the transit officers.

The nose of the train crept forward. The engineer stood at attention with his eyes wide and hair askew. The vehicle reached the point Rog requested and drew to a gentle stop.

He took a deep breath realizing he and Baker had not discussed what to do with the doors once in the station. Rog willed the idea to his buddy. Right as he prepared to take his phone out, Rog heard the opening indicator bell followed by a resounding crash.

Rog leapt toward the door which was still a little inside the tunnel. He had visions of Talker escaping solo. He wanted to get between Talker and his assumed freedom.

Rog ran into a barrel chested guy with a blond crewcut in a dark navy business suit. Instinctually, Rog grabbed him and held him in place before realizing he had the wrong guy.

"What the-"

The business man was interrupted by a scream. Though big and imposing, he looked around in a panic. He wore an expression of someone about to burst into tears.

"He had a knife," the business man blubbered.

"I'll take care of it," Rog said.

He tried to ease the other man out of the way. He quickly shepherded him into the front compartment with the engineer.

With the crisis averted, Rog headed into the tunnel. He spotted movement further down the train. Ignoring what it might be, he ducked his head into the first car. Rog saw no sign of Talker or the Librarian. He found the handful of passengers staring at him with alarm on their faces.

"Where did they go?" Rog snapped.

A few people pointed toward him. One of the passengers, a young man with eyeliner and blue black hair, gestured back up the tunnel.

"Thanks. Stay here until the train is in the station." Rog yelled back at the engineer. "Call Baker and tell him the guy's still got her and is taking her back to their departure point."

Without waiting for a reply, Rog turned and sprinted down the narrow gap between the train and the tunnel. He banged both his arms a few times. Rog started counting cars.

Reaching the end and peering into the darkness, he heard the sound of someone scrambling up the tracks. Rog stayed silent not wanting to spook his quarry.

His eyes slowly adjusted. He saw a taller figure hunch over a little one. Rog assumed Talker sought to intimidate the Librarian to continue toward the previous station. He supposed Talker could be doing something more horrible. With an eerie stillness in the air, he put anything too untoward out of his mind and crept forward slowly.

Rog felt his heart leap into his throat at a blood curdling scream. Rog assumed the Librarian had come to harm and broke into a run pushing down the fear welling up in him.

"This can't happen again," he muttered to himself. "I won't let it. Not again."

Pushing aside his fear of the situation, Rog broke into a sprint toward the combatants. He heard a second scream. He thought it sounded weaker than the first as though the energy behind the initial cry had ebbed away. He picked up his pace.

Drawing nearer, Rog called out, "Get away from her."

Once close enough to see, he gasped with surprise, fighting

to understand the scene. Rog opened his mouth to say something else and then closed it as quickly.

"I'm fine, Dear," a feral voice rumbled out of the towering form. "Though that's very sweet of you to be worried about me. I've been taking care of myself for quite a while now."

Rog fought to keep the pizza in his stomach as the hulking beast with the extended, blood covered snout spoke. Looking at the ground where he had expected to see the prone from of the Librarian, Rog spied Talker with a stricken look of surprise on his face as he continued to hold his ineffectual knife with a bent blade in his hand.

"What.... what are you doing?"

"Why I'm just cleaning up this mess," the sleek predator said. "I'll be honest, he's far tastier than I would have guessed. Though I will say I'm disappointed you intervened, Dear. His friend. Hulk was it? Had quite a bit more meat. I'm guessing his muscles were nicely marbled."

"You," Rog said. "You killed him."

"Very much so." The big lupine creature let out a burbling, mirthless laugh. "You're a sweet boy, but you don't strike me as too bright."

Rog reached for a gun he no longer carried. He took a fighting stance and hoped his training, in addition to giving him a leaner physique since losing his job, provided him with enough hand-to-hand combat skills to take on whatever the Librarian had changed into.

He saw a pitying look come across her face. He wondered if she would pounce on him like she had with Talker. He was surprised when she bent back down opening her jaws before crushing Talker's throat. Rog felt the spray of blood and viscera start its slow trek down his face. He held the ready stance taught to him by his sensei, ignoring the sticky dripping sensation.

"Hey," Rog shouted at the thing he could not stop thinking of as the Librarian. "I don't know what you are-"

"What I am?" the blood slicked beast said through a mouthful of Talker. "Why, dear, I was trying to give you a way out. I know you think of yourself as some sort of gallant knight. A defender of the weak. But even you should know that not everyone is weak." She finished chewing and swallowing the bite in her mouth. "In fact, some of us are quite strong and it feels very good."

Rog shuddered a little at the ghastly grin she shared with him. As he assessed her size and strength, Rog hoped the engineer had called Baker.

"You're right about that and I'm sure he wasn't a model citizen." Rog dipped his head toward Talker. "But even he didn't deserve that."

She bent down taking another bite. In the near darkness, her eyes flashed a full grey. She tilted her head, swallowed and met Rog's gaze with those withering pools.

"Fortunately, these are not decisions you get to make. I'm giving you one more chance to leave. I promise you this will satisfy me for a while, so you won't have to worry about me."

Rog felt the chill of vague recollection enter his mind and chase the growing dread through the rest of his body like an electrical current. He swallowed against the lump growing in his throat.

"When was the last time you did this?" Rog asked.

His mouth had a thick dryness like dehydration or extreme nervousness. He kept the poise positioned. Rog hoped he would be ready to strike if it came to that.

The Librarian cocked her now monstrous head to one side as though hearing a distant sound. Her eyes locked on his.

"I was wrong about you." Her voice sounded like a concrete

mixer with mostly dry cement banging around inside. "Were you hoping to keep me busy until the cavalry got here, dear?"

Rog could not help but feel like a rabbit being gauged by a much bigger predator. He set his jaw. His mind leapt to the idea that help was on its way. He needed to hold on, that was all.

"I don't know what you're talking about. I asked you a question." He nodded down to Talker. "You basically told me this is what you do. So when did you do this last? When did you feed and where?"

As with Hulk, Rog never saw the blow coming knocking him on his ass. After he skipped a short distance and looked up at the concave roof of the old tunnel, Rog registered the pain passing through his body radiating from his chest. Rog acknowledged the distraction for Hulk's successful blow, but attributed the Librarian's incalculable speed as her advantage.

He coughed. His eyes went out of focus. Rog feared losing consciousness. He pushed aside any childish fears of being eaten by the beast because they seemed to be fully engaged in the consumption of what they could of Talker.

Rog sat up triggering greater pain spreading through his body. He coughed louder. Turning over and getting a knee under him, Rog tried to get himself upright. He kept his eyes off the hideous events going on further down the tunnel.

He rose and took a few unsteady steps toward the hunched figure. Rog guessed she was trying to finish and get away before what she heard arrived. He looked around for something to attack with. His eyes landed on a piece of rebar with bricks and concrete attached like an ancient mace. His fingers closed around the metal and hefted it.

Seeing him brandish the makeshift weapon, the beast gurgled dangerously, "I'm giving you a chance, knight. You don't think my kind does this very often, do you? You need to run."

Hearing the admonishment, Rog stumbled a few more steps forward. He swung overhead with all his might until the Librarian stopped the descent with an impossibly huge claw. He watched her crush the piece of masonry, leaving him only a bar of steel.

She looked at him with her baleful eyes. She stalked through the dust of the exploding cement. The Librarian blinked her eyes and snapped her jaws in rapid succession.

"You are entirely too dogged to be allowed to live," she growled gutterally. "I have seen people, even those who thought themselves braver than anyone else, flee."

"I guess I'm not that smart. You should surrender before something bad happens."

"You mean before your precious reinforcements arrive? You should know something." Her menacing form seemed to fill all the space in the tunnel back toward the other station. "They're still a long way off. Your kind has never been skilled at truly hunting. You can't be quiet. Especially when you want to be."

Rog saw her spring forward. Recalling some of his early lessons about falling to avoid direct attacks, Rog acted before his mind could stop him. His body dropped, intending to grapple her to the ground.

She flew at him and tried to alter her trajectory. Her claws dipped toward his falling body.

He felt the burn as his jacket and shirt opened along with the tender skin under it. Rog heard a growling yell. He thought it must be the Librarian furious battle cry. Feeling the rough vibration of his vocal cords, he let the surprise of his pained cry wash over him. He watched the blood well up from the three furrows which did not seem nearly deep enough to cause such a level of pain.

Rog pushed himself to one knee again. He looked around in the darkness for the Librarian. He thought he heard sounds to his right, but realized the noises were being made by something far smaller than the beast.

He turned to his left in time to see a big open talon coming at him. He dodged the blow only to be sent back to a single knee. He quickly used the technique that laid Hulk out. Rog drove a blunted fist into the thing's crotch unsure of the damage that might be done. He gave a small, satisfied smile at the bellow of pain.

Rog moved in close and landed two more blows to its tender bit and then applied all his strength to an uppercut. In his mind, he saw himself like the scrappy underdog taking out the bruiser with a single blow. Instead, his hand met what he thought must be bone crunching steel since his fist throbbed as though shattered.

He was shocked when the beast staggered back. Rog was not sure why. He could not imagine being that effective. As the Librarian towered over him with an odd expression on her monstrous face, he heard the strange sound like a distant popping before her left eye exploded like a kernel of popcorn.

She staggered for a moment with a look of confusion. She let out an airy growl. With nothing left to say, the Librarian collapsed on him in a heap.

Rog lost consciousness underneath the thing. He thought that he must be about to die from his wound or the weight of her laying under him. He dreamed of this all being over. Whatever she was, he was sure she would not kill again.

He woke in the hospital to find his wounds dressed and hooked up to a bunch of machines. He saw a man about ten years older than him with a hangdog expression sitting in the chair flipping through a magazine.

"Well, about time you woke up."

"Baker?" Rog croaked. "What... what happened?"

"You saved a bunch of people is what happened," the transit worker said with a lopsided smile. "You did good, Buddy."

"I didn't do anything."

"Yeah, you sure as hell did."

Rog reached down to touch the dressing on his chest wound. "What... what was that?"

"Oh, that was a werewolf," Baker said casually. "This has been her feeding grounds for almost 100 years."

"What?"

Baker stood up still smiling. "Don't try to figure it all out." He pulled out a card and placed it on the rolling table beside the bed. "Get better and when you do, come there. It'll all be clearer."

When Baker left, Rog reached for the card wincing in pain. He looked at the odd script. He shook his head because the words did not make sense to him.

"What the hell is the Bastille Society?"

HIS TIME OF THE MONTH

BY KEITH 'DOC' RAYMOND

Sigrún walked Zorn and Blaze over the tundra in the twilight before the long Icelandic night. Spotting a group of arctic hares, Zorn broke his leash to savage them. Sigrún had a strong stomach, but she still turned away from the slaughter. Blaze kept pulling her towards it, eager to join the fray, but she held him, throwing the leash over her shoulder.

The cracking of bones, growling, and tearing of muscle became too much. She dry heaved and attempted to move upwind, struggling with Blaze. The beast's eyes flared red with blood lust. She was losing ground when Zorn trotted back, his muzzle covered in crimson. Blaze licked the remains away from Zorn's mouth, sniffing deeply, bathing in the massacre.

After the face bath, Zorn looked up at Sigrún. She squatted and accepted his apology as he nuzzled her neck, his fragrant fur brushing her cheek. The depth of love was so sweet, Sigrún released Blaze to finish up what Zorn left behind. The woman and wolf embraced, holding each other, sharing a feeling few would ever know.

"I suppose it's better than feeding on humans," she whispered.

Zorn nuzzled her again, crying like a puppy.

"At the rate you're going, I won't be able to keep you in leashes!"

He growled, turning to look for Blaze. The malamute was picking through the scraps, wagging his thick tail. The alpha male made it easy for Blaze. A retired wheel dog from a mushing team, Blaze was used to taking the leftovers. Enjoyed it, actually. Plus, Sigrún and Zorn were great masters, and he got to sleep inside!

Zorn howled, drawing Blaze's attention. The howl said 'time to go.' The malamute trotted back, dragging his leash through the muck. Sigrún picked it up, and they headed back toward Reykjavik as darkness fell. She had to get Zorn in before he changed. The temperatures were not conducive to a naked man in the snow.

The folks in town gave Sigrún and her beasts a wide berth. It made them nervous to see the wolf off-leash, his broken lead dragging. The wolf was taller than a man, and the residual blood on his muzzle did nothing to reassure them. But he heeled by the woman's side. Alone, she seemed no less danger-ous, and looked like a shield maiden from the Viking times.

People wondered why they only saw this wolf during the full moon and joked that it was probably a werewolf. They were happy he appeared only occasionally, because having an animal like that in the city meant children weren't safe. Despite their concerns, they admired the trio, and tourists gawked.

Sigrún was tall with carved features, muscular from chop-ping wood. Callused hands and long dirty blond hair gave her a proud air. She lived a solitary life except for her man, Zorn. If anyone asked why he wasn't around, she ignored them.

Reaching their turf house in Reykjavik, Sigrún noticed her

wolf shedding heavily. She pushed open the door and the two beasts surged in around her. Blaze went to his usual spot. She watched Zorn's transformation as if for the first time.

His heavily bearded face, bushy hair, and lean body hid a strength that made her shiver. At the very least, he turned her on. Mates for several hundred years, they moved often to disguise their lack of ageing.

"Hello lover," Zorn barked, coughing out white fur and scratching at residual patches.

"Did you enjoy the hunt?" Sigrún asked.

"Every time."

"Well, Blaze still needs to eat and so do I," she said, lifting a twenty kilo bag of kibble. She poured some out into his bowl. The malamute stood with a grunt and walked over, sniffed, then ate. Zorn turned his nose up at the kibble and settled back down on a pile of skins, transforming back into his wolf form to sleep.

As he snored, Sigrún poured out some reindeer blood from a jug in the refrigerator, shoving the mug into the microwave. Pulling it out when it reached body temperature, she avoided letting the oven bell ring so the two beasts could sleep. Blaze already settled in next to Zorn.

Sigrún eased into a chair by the fire and sipped from the steaming mug. A scene of domestic bliss considering the monsters that lived there. She was dozing off when a gust of wind rattled the rafters. The animals woke instantly, ears pricked. Zorn sniffed the air and growled.

Another gust of wind and a single thud struck the front door. Blaze barked, and Zorn jumped up, his fur rising on his neck. Sigrún stood and faced the menace. The door flew inward and bounced off the wall as a tall Polish Prince entered. He slammed the door behind him and marched into Sigrún's arms, only to be pushed away.

"Stashu! You're not welcome here! This is Zorn's time of the month. His year," Sigrún said. Despite the warning, she drew him back and hugged him. He kissed her on both cheeks and stepped away.

"Wizard privilege!" he gushed. "But I have reason to be here. Word from the Tatras is they are hunting down werewolves."

Zorn transformed from a wolf into a werewolf to challenge Sigrún's second husband. Wizard or not, Stashu was in his territory. Warning or not, he would pay. Blaze backed up, not wanting any part of the fight. Sigrún stepped between her husbands, sensing the impending attack. Zorn panted, saliva running down his canines.

"Easy, down boy," warned Stashu.

This only infuriated him. Zorn howled, deafening in the enclosed space. Sigrún eased out of the way, realising the fight was inevitable. Stashu swirled his hands asynchronously, generating a protection spell. An opalescent energy egg engulfed him. Zorn swiped at it, pushing through, and his claws would have grated flesh if Stashu had not slipped away.

He appeared behind Zorn, but the werewolf smelled Stashu and leaped backwards, butting` the wizard into the fire. Stashu cried out, hair burning, and teleported outside to roll in the snow, going invisible. The burst of magic shook snow off the roof. The crash of icicles telling Zorn where Stashu appeared. Now the wizard was in the werewolf's element.

Running straight through the door, he pounced on Stashu, pinning him in a drift. Saliva dripped on the now visible wizard's face, air bellowing from Zorn's lungs. He bit down on the man's head, but Stashu shrank into a mouse and skittered away. Zorn's jaws snapped shut on the frigid air.

Sigrún leaned out of the destroyed entrance, hands on hips. "Are you done, Zorn?! Now you can fix the bloody door!"

The werewolf cowered, as if beaten. Glancing around, he looked for the mouse. Satisfied he left, Zorn reverted to a man, walked to the shed, and started his chainsaw. In short order, he cut boards, lashed them together, and made a serviceable door replacement.

All the while, Sigrún stared in disdain at the man wolf. Still, she wrapped him in a polar bear coat, her eyes glowing from her own between the collars. When he finally shut the new front door, she asked, "Did you hear anything Stashu said?"

"Some warning about hunts in the Tatras Mountains."

"Werewolf hunts. We may not be safe here."

"If the silver market hadn't bottomed out, they wouldn't be going after my kind."

She smiled, answering, "What about your family? They are in the Tatras."

"Left long ago."

"They have trackers. They might come after us and your den."

"So, what do you suggest? The Americas?"

"Good eating there, though definitely high in cholesterol."

"Something to consider."

"Now, where did you chase Stashu off to?"

* * *

A computer hack of the hotel registries in Reykjavik turned Stashu up fairly quickly. Sigrún went to check on him while Zorn went out hunting with Blaze. When Stashu opened the door, it pleased him to see Sigrún alone.

"I apologize for Zorn," she began.

"No need. I know the rules of our marriage triangle. I violated them. But I was looking out for him, and you."

"How have you been?"

"Lonely. Big cold castles and young witches no longer satisfy."

"I didn't know you still indulged. I thought you gave up on covens once we married."

"I tried, really. But they kept calling. There are so few of us left."

"A clever excuse. I'm not buying it!" Sigrún said with a devilish grin.

"You've got me! Still, I miss you terribly. Even restocked the refrigerator for your return. Some choice virgin blood..."

"Hmm, young boys!"

"You don't know how uneasy that makes me?"

"You're safe. Besides, I know for certain you aren't a virgin!" she said. "Now, what about this werewolf hunt?"

"It's bad, Sigrún. There's not enough wolfs-bane remaining for spells. The hunters are ravaging the hills. Setting out traps. They've even caught vampires and drugging them with aconite to use as bait. Once they capture a paralyzed werewolf, they restrain and flay them."

"But why? And why now?"

"Word has it, a Maltese prince lost his daughter? First, the wolf seduced her, then dragged her off to feed to his children. Double damage, both to honor and love."

"What werewolf is so indiscreet?"

"Perhaps he didn't know who she was? Or he couldn't resist her beauty and the taste of her flesh."

"The beast!" she said. Then smiled at the thought of being savaged by Zorn. Self-consciously, she touched her neck where Zorn's recent scars were fading.

"Oh, the hunters caught him all right. Killed the cubs, too. But that didn't stop them..."

"Knowing Zorn, he won't run from the fire, but towards it!"

"You'd best encourage him to leave the continent. They are traveling in groups, these knights. Killing, burning, and salting the ground behind them," Stashu said, using reverse psychology to draw his rival into the trap.

A howl in the forest made them turn away from each other. So Sigrún missed Stashu's true intent, thinking he honestly cared about Zorn.

"It's him. I better go." She headed toward the exit, missing Stashu's grin.

When she arrived back home, the first thing the wolf did was sniff her crotch. He wagged his tail a little and backed up. Sigrún apologised to Zorn for visiting Stashu, but before he could leave to attack the wizard once more, she told him Stashu had already checked out. Zorn turned back, gold eyes flashing, searching her face for deceit.

Later, Zorn padded after Sigrún as she went for a cup of tea in a nearby cafe. The wolf jumped up on the bench beside her, and Sigrún filled him in about Stashu's warning. The wolf tilted his head right and left, growled a little, showed teeth, and whined occasionally.

A Texas tourist watched Sigrun's conversation with the beast, bemusedly. She turned to her husband, hungover from Aquavit and jet lag, and said, "Isn't that something, Hank? Them carrying on that way."

"That there woman is too purty to be demented."

"You mind your P's and Q's, Hank."

"Yes, Ma'am! But hey, you brought it up."

"So let's see... we have a busy day. First, we have the Blue Lagoon, then Seljalandsfoss, then–"

Sigrún finished her tea and rose. Zorn jumped down and walked beside her.

"Nice dog you got there," noted Hank.

"Wolf! And he's not mine. Found him in the wild," she said in English.

"Now you quit!" said the wife to Hank. "The guide told us not to disturb the locals."

Zorn growled as they left.

"See what I mean."

* * *

They took the midnight flight from Reykjavik to Gdansk. Sigrún packed what weapons she could into her luggage. Zorn packed hunting clothes. Taking his human form, he smelled musky after his day of hunting. The gamey smell was difficult to wash off.

Settling into their seats, a large bearded man boarded the plane. He looked a little too long at Sigrún and Zorn, setting off their alarm bells, then he sat several rows in front of them. She whispered to Zorn, and agreeing under his breath, he answered, "Tracker."

An hour into the flight, the bearded man rose, heading back to the bathroom. Most of the people on the red eye flight slept. Zorn looked around, noting the flight staff behind the curtain up in first class. He stood and walked toward the back of the plane, seeing the bearded man duck into a toilet.

Standing in front of the locked door, he listened. Zorn grabbed the handle and shoved it down, breaking the lock, and went inside, closing the door behind him. The man was toying with a satellite phone, about to make a call.

He saw Zorn and chuckled, "Hey dude, I'm not part of the mile high club."

Zorn grabbed him around his thick neck, his hand morphing into a paw, black claws sprouting. He lifted him up against the back wall, right off the toilet, and choked him until his eyes bulged and his tongue lolled. His face went blue, then gray, head dropping. Zorn let go of him and stepped out.

Back at his seat, he turned to Sigrún, and said, "I left you a snack in the back."

She saw one toilet sign that wasn't engaged and nodded. She slid past him, following his scent to the toilet. The bearded man was still unconscious, but wouldn't be for long.

She pulled down his pants and was just about to feed when the door behind her opened. The young woman standing there took in the scene. Seeing Sigrún on her knees, she came to the wrong conclusion. To add to her imagination, the bearded man rolled his head around and moaned.

"Sorry, next time better lock the door," she said, then added, "Have fun." Closing the door, the young woman warned someone else off.

Sigrún dug her fangs into his femoral artery and drank from the fountain quickly and efficiently until his heart stopped and his blood pressure dropped to zero. Then she pulled his pants up and left him there. She checked her makeup in the mirror, wiped her lips, and picked up the sat phone.

Walking back to her seat, she licked her lips. The young woman touched her arm as she passed, seeing the tongue swipe. "Enjoy the rest of your flight," she said, and winked. Sigrún burped, and both women chuckled.

She handed the phone to Zorn, saying, "All sorted. Now let's see who his friends are?"

* * *

Landing before sunrise, they took a taxi to a hotel. Choosing a room in the back, out of direct sunlight, they settled in for the day. Using the local Wi-Fi, Zorn tracked the few numbers displayed on the phone.

The one that looked promising was from the Maltese Taxidermy Federation. They had a chapter in Poznan, southwest of Gdansk. It must be where the hunters met. The new Templars turned their attention from holy to unholy pursuits. Zorn planned to make them pay.

At dinner, while Zorn was tearing through a tough steak, Sigrún paged through that morning's newspaper. She had no appetite after her meal the night before. Of course, they reported the death onboard the flight, listed as a 'heart attack.' In another story, she found several hunting accidents in the forests of Poland with signs of wolf attacks.

The article reported that the number of cases during this hunting season was significantly higher than usual. Of particular note, the forest rangers found the dead hunters without rifles and a naked man stabbed at one site. They suspected the 'accidents' involved thefts of their weapons. The police asked for help from the public, and were deploying trackers.

When she related the contents of the article to Zorn, he shrugged. Clearly, werewolves killed the hunters. Stashu was right to warn them. Sigrún wondered whether her other husband was even in Iceland. Perhaps the bearded man was a warlock who took Stashu's appearance to lure Zorn.

She closed the newspaper, saying, "Zorn, you can't go into the forest now. The moon is out of phase. You'll be vulnerable."

"I don't care. A bullet will take them down as effectively as teeth."

"I care. We are fighting a posse. We need every advantage. I suggest we use the time to gather intel."

He nodded, seeing her logic. "Off to Poznan, then."

* * *

Taking the night train, they checked into a Poznan hotel early in the morning. Looking over a city map, Sigrún located the taxidermy shop.

As he unpacked, he said, "I need to get in there."

"You can't. They'll spot and kill you before you even inquire. I doubt if even I could get in there. If they sent a tracker after you, no doubt they know who I am."

"Then what?"

"Find me a body."

"You want me to kill someone right off?!"

"No, no, an animal body. Something the taxidermist can work on."

Together, they prowled the alleys before sunrise. It wasn't long before Zorn sniffed out a black cat by a dumpster. He picked it up as if it would give him rabies. The look of distaste on his face was plain.

"What now?" he asked.

"You'll figure it out," Sigrún answered, and winked at him.

He stared incredulously as Sigrún exploded, transforming herself into a cloud of mosquitoes. He looked at the cat in his fist, its mouth open, and the swarm swept inside. Once the mosquitoes disappeared into the cat, he closed its mouth just as the sun rose. Orange light sprayed down the cobblestone streets of the old town.

A group of boys jostled each other, running toward a bakery at the corner.

"Hey you! Want to make some money?" Zorn called out in bad Polish. He held up a wad of cash in one hand and the dead cat in the other.

"Ain't nothing good comes from playing with a dead cat," one said.

"What? You want me to give that to my teacher?!" another teased.

Zorn pointed to the smallest boy in the group. "You! I give you ten zloty if you take this cat to the Maltese Taxidermist over on Zygmuntowska."

The boy approached Zorn, glad someone acknowledged him for once.

"Ask him," nodding toward the taxidermist, "to stuff this cat for you."

"What's his name?"

"You mean the cat? Fluffy."

"Okay, I do it. For twenty."

"You drive a hard bargain."

"Drive? How do you drive a bargain?"

"Forget it! And here's a deposit for the man."

"Hey Jakub, what you do with dead cat?" one of the older boys asked.

"Make money."

Jakub walked off whistling, heading for the taxidermist shop. Zorn followed discreetly, stopping at the corner. He hid behind the building and watched to be sure Jakub did what he was told. Jakub rang the doorbell. The store was closed. Rang again. Then again.

A fat gray-haired man came to the door, rubbing his eyes, wearing an old nightshirt. He opened it with the ring of a small bell above the door. Zorn couldn't hear what the boy said, but he held up the dead cat, and pushed money into his doughy fist. The man shook his head and carried the cat inside, while Jakub ran back toward the bakery.

Ten minutes later, the door opened, and Zorn saw Sigrun's pale, smoking hand beckon him inside. Zorn looked about, then approached, seeing a small sign in the shop's window at the bottom corner. 'Society Meeting Here Tonight.'

Inside, Zorn saw the taxidermist sprawled on the floor covered in welts from mosquito bites. Shrunken and pale, she drained him of blood. Death by a thousand cuts would have been merciful compared to the death she inflicted. First the itching, then the pain everywhere, followed by fatigue, weakness, and finally loss of consciousness and death.

Sigrún looked at Zorn and said, "You think I'm the monster? His blood memories carried horrors, gruesome murders of your kind. Death so terrible, I'm still nauseous."

"But did you find anything of value?"

"Oh, yes."

"The Templars are hunting werewolves globally. Hunting them to extinction. The Poznan forest is one of the last dens of any size or significance left."

"They have a meeting tonight," Zorn said, concerned about the werewolf slaughter.

"Yes, I know. But you must reach out to your brothers. They are planning a hunt. A big one. A final solution."

"What about you? You can't go out now."

"I'll remain in the shadows here and listen in. You get rid of the body, then go."

Zorn nodded to Sigrún and dragged the taxidermist into a back alley, tossing him into a dumpster, then left. This news was more than worrisome. It infuriated him. Making them pay wasn't enough for these Templars. He intended to make them suffer. Sigrun's devotion to him and his kind always amazed him. But then, perhaps their next campaign was to go after vampires. He refused to lose his woman.

* * *

On the other side of Poznan, in a basement pub aptly named the Wolf's Lair, Zorn was drinking a pint of Killa piwo (a Pilz beer from a local craft brewery aptly named Voodoo) at the bar.

He sniffed the air and waited. When he smelled the first of his kind, he turned towards the door.

Five bearded men, eyes flaring gold on seeing an uninvited werewolf, stepped forward. Zorn violated their territory. He knew it, but he didn't care. He might get mauled, but his message took priority. This den was under threat, and they were on edge. The Alpha of their clan marched straight toward Zorn.

Zorn raised his hands. "Hey, I don't want any trouble."

"Trouble found you, Cub!"

"I'm here to help."

They laughed. "What can a lone wolf do against a pack, or the hunters out there?" barked the Alpha.

"I have information and a plan."

"A plan, do you?" The Alpha turned to his pack, then whipped a backhand straight into Zorn's face, knocking him to the floor, ordering the attack.

Zorn was getting it from all sides, but they couldn't change into wolf form. Their fists and boots wouldn't kill a werewolf. Just bring blood and pain.

"That's enough!" A deep voice bellowed loudly from the front door.

The Alpha looked up, while the others continued to attack Zorn. This time the real Stashu stood there, wearing a bearskin coat and leather pants. His hands were swirling purple balls of lightning before him. The barkeep reached for a shotgun, but before he could grab it, Stashu fired the spheres of power at the pack. Each ball struck and flattened all the wolves and the barkeep.

Zorn lay there panting, "Stashu! Thank Christ."

"Bent but not broken," Stashu surmised. "Sigrún said I might find you here. I sensed her presence in Poland."

"So you never came to us in Iceland?" Zorn asked, standing

with difficulty and brushing himself off. He glanced down at the pack at his feet.

"Why would I? I hate tundra and tourists! And don't worry about those wolves. They'll be up in no time."

"I owe you a beer."

"Finally! Thought you'd never ask."

Zorn righted his stool, and Stashu joined him. The werewolf reached around the taps and pulled two Killa piwo for them, handing one to Stashu. Zorn noted Stashu's widow's peak, and his long black hair. He smelled like tree sap. Looking more like a lumberjack than a wizard, Zorn noted his thick shoulders and muscled arms.

When the Alpha regained consciousness, Zorn stood over him, sharing what he knew about the real hunters, the Maltese Templars, and his plan to deal with them. Stashu nodded and shared his association with Zorn and Sigrún with the other wolves. Stashu's Polish, his magic, the plan and the piwo he offered the Alpha gave them all hope. The den knew about the slaughter of other packs by the knights. But having a vampire and wizard by their side improved their odds.

Now all they had to do was to prepare and wait for the next full moon to counterattack.

Philippe, Captain of the Templar Knights, peaked over the berm at the wolf's den. Many she-wolves and their cubs meandered a hundred meters away. He looked right and left at the row of knights at his command. Laying on their bellies, they waited for the signal to attack. They exchanged chain mail for body armor. But instead of modern weapons, they had crossbows with silver arrows. It would not do to conduct a war within earshot of the city.

Philippe turned to Andrzej, his second in command, "What was the name of that boy who tipped us off about the werewolves again?"

"Jakub."

"His coordinates were accurate. It looks quiet. They'll never expect a sneak attack during a full moon. They don't even look prepared."

Andrzej tilted his head up at the silvery orb spraying light on the forest. It seemed foolhardy to him. She-wolves were the more deadly of the werewolf genders. But then Philippe was a Templar with many victories behind him, and this was the last big den in Europe. One and done.

"What's this?" Andrzej asked.

Stepping into the beams of moonlight, on the field between the berm and the den, a lone figure. At first, a silhouette. Then white wings, a shining breastplate, a shield, and a battle ax.

"A bloody Viking!" one knight uttered and chuckled.

"A Valkyrie, you idiot!" said another. The knights laughed at her bravado.

She struck her shield with her ax. "I am Sigrún, daughter of King Hogni." Struck her shield again, "Wife of Helgi, Stashu and Zorn," another strike with a step forward, "Resurrected as Kara by the blood of Dracula," strike and another step forward, "I live to do battle. My battles are legendary..." another step forward. She recited every battle she fought, striking her shield with her battle ax, stepping forward after each one.

The display hypnotized the knights, not only by her speech, but by her beauty. Behind her, an eerie gloom appeared. A darkness hiding the den created by Stashu, a veil behind which the wolves transformed.

Philippe stood to face Sigrún. "And what can one Viking do against a legion of knights?"

The others stood and leveled their crossbows at her. Then a

series of low growls behind the knights alerted Andrzej to the danger.

"Fire!" Philippe ordered.

Several hundred men loosed their arrows at Sigrún and the wolf's den. She moved so quickly; it seemed she simply disappeared. Sigrún ran before the skirmish line. Using her shield, she knocked down all the arrows in mid-flight, then returned to her place in the center. She raised her ax in the air and brought it down.

The werewolves attacked the knights in a pincer move from both directions, behind and in front. The rending of muscle, sinew flying, bones cracking, and the dying screams of knights and wolves echoed through the night. Templars trapped in a kill box swore as the battle raged on.

Zorn emerged from the fray, muzzle bloody, dripping from multiple wounds when he spotted the Captain. He stalked toward Philippe as the man thrust a silver sword through a she-wolf. She landed on the ground, transforming back into a woman. Even dead, she was beautiful. Zorn bristled with anger.

"Try someone in your own weight class," Zorn growled out.

"Por favor, bring it," Philippe answered, sweeping the blood from his sword, arms open in an invitation. His smile, hungry.

Zorn leaped at the knight, and the Captain parried, his blade swishing through the air in an arc. Zorn howled as the tip raked his belly, steam coming from the wound. The werewolf landed behind him, rolling back onto his feet. Gripping the wound, he yelped as it burned.

The two opponents panted at each other, glaring menace. Zorn held his belly, while blood ran down the Templar's scalp from a claw swipe. Philippe wiped the blood from his eye and stomped forward. "I will kill you for that, you monster!"

Zorn backed away from the knight as his sword sang,

scything the air, the silver gleaming in the moonlight. The werewolf was weaker than he let on, suffering from his injuries. But he was determined to kill this madman whose thirst for his kind decimated their ranks. Even if it cost Zorn his own life.

Behind the beast was a well. Seeing it, Philippe drove the werewolf towards it, hoping to force the animal to fall in and to his death. Zorn backed to the bricks, grabbed a bucket full of water, swinging it at the knight, as the only weapon at hand. The Captain laughed at the sight of a werewolf with only a bucket to defend himself against an armed Templar.

Philippe charged forward as Stashu flew overhead. The wizard sent a swirl of purple light into the water. The powerful alchemy changing it into nitric acid. Zorn sensed the change, but used the bucket to deflect the sword as it cut the air. Its arc slipping harmlessly past.

The Captain backhanded the blade, and Zorn leaped onto the edge of the well to avoid it, while tossing the acid at the knight. It sloshed over the blade and onto his armor, sizzling. A drop hit Philippe's cheek, burning instantly, raising a blister. The knight staggered back for a moment, touching his face in surprise.

Then Philippe laughed, drunk with bloodlust and, in a berserker's frenzy, yelled, "You hoped to defeat me with fire water? That was your last mistake, animale!" And he redoubled his attack, his sword collecting moonlight as it flashed.

Except the change had already taken place. Zorn grabbed the well's rope roller and flipped away as Philippe swung his sword like an ax, hoping to cleave the werewolf in half. The sword shattered as it struck the bricks on the side of the well. The metal converted to white powdery silver nitrate by the acid.

Taking two steps back in horror, the pommel of Philippe's sword glanced off his armor, and it crumbled, falling off him in pieces. The sudden advantage put Zorn on the offensive. He leaped at the knight, soaring over his head and twisted, landing behind him. The Captain turned his head, but he was too late to fend off the attack.

The werewolf, in one swipe, clawed the skin from Philippe's back, then ripped his spine out with his jaws. He whipped it in the air, rattling this bony snake of torn nerves. The Captain dropped. The Templar undeniably dead.

This was the last kill on the field, an act of triumph. The den sensed it was over. A hundred werewolves howled, blood streaming from their jaws, spattering their coats. The war ended and a feast lay before them.

Sigrún and Stashu climbed onto the berm and stared down at the killing field. Admiring the victory, they hugged. Sigrún, worried, stepped back, looking for Zorn among the dead.

Zorn raced toward them from the well, shouting, "We will never forget this night, Sigrún! Stashu, celebrate with us. You're one of us now. Come join the pack!"

The werewolves lifted their heads, and even the cubs howled once more. Their song echoing through the land.

In Poznan, the people looked warily toward the forest. Then up at the moon, quaking in fear.

KOOSHTI LOLLIPOP SHERBET CUNT

BY KATIE NESS

Kooshti: Romani word for 'Very Good'

Lollipop: An anglicised form of Romani 'Loli Phabai' which means 'red apple'-It was first a Roma tradition to sell candied apples on a stick.

Sherbet: Originally a Persian word meaning 'Iced fruity drink' that included herbs and flowers.

Cunt: Originally **NOT** an offensive word, Potentially originated from the name 'Kunti' who was an ancient Hindu Goddess of fertility and wisdom called 'The great Yoni of the Universe'–Yoni also meaning 'Vagina' in Sanskrit.

PART ONE

P ink haired, frizzy and fizzing; a pale Pleiadian blush of a woman crosses the road of blinking traffic lights. She is in a rush to catch a train to the countryside. Deep in thought over the variety of factors contributing to her series of collisions in her late-thirty-something-bland-life she doesn't see the taxi, a large reverberating black wingless beetle swivels past her. The only flavours in this monochrome existence are: Dark humoured memes shared on Instagram stories on an insomnia riddled 3 am Thursday, her hair that she is constantly dyeing in an assortment of colours, (last month it was alien green), and her marmalade cat who ignores her with a Taylor Swift side-eyed petulance.

Stephanie orbits a rusty, moss crocheted bridge heralded by street lamps gleaming upon the train station tracks. Tired of the cycle of bad luck, she wonders 'Did I break a mirror when I was a kid?... Fuck this shit!.' Too many years of skies sinking stones in her lungs, too many fault lines have broken her heart into shards. The weight of everything, the turmoil of sweeping scavenging winds. Cast out and cursed like a bloodshot smudge, like a moth whose wings were sewn back on. She cannot stand straight, she bends, tilting like the earth and uprooting in the gale–This is hurt that her yoga class on Saturday afternoons can not fix. In those cold minutes she recalled all the years of unease and fear. Reaching platform six she misses her train by two minutes. Leaning into a stained glass window to light a cigarette, she mutters "Fuck my life" and sends sardonic text messages to a friend before her mobile died.

Stef: I missed my fucking train. I'm the bitch of bad luck.

Rob van Riot: You are the Damsel of Despair my dear.

Stef: Rob, I'm falling apart. I'm tired of all this shit. I'm cursed. I also find it hard to distinguish between paranoia and anxiety these days. Guilt is just down to the bad choices I make. Might play my 'Hate myself and want to die 2023 mix'?

Rob: Evergreen death comet.

Stef: I used to think I was evergreen. Now I'm Nevegrin.

Rob: Pantone.

Stef: Keeping my pant-on has always been part of the problem.

Rob: So... My neon void surfer, when's your next train?

Stef: Twenty minutes. Fuck my phone's about to die. I'll message you when I'm up north.

Stephanie was a misanthropic and pessimistic woman. She lived alone in a rented flat, with some houseplants, her sullen cat and a mattress on the floor surrounded by books and unwashed coffee mugs. She worked in a local pub called 'The Kelpie's Noose,' had aspirations to be a yoga teacher and wore vintage rock T-shirts, skinny jeans and leopard print knickers. Stephanie could rip off a beer bottle with her teeth, balance in Bakasana for a minute and enjoyed skinny dipping in winter. A neon wildcat caged, cantankerous and complex with layers of percolating emotions, some spiritual, others tortured.

Anemone bright, Stephanie was beguiling yet riddled with self loathing, given to sulking and there was a bitterness to her, a bitterness as hardened and fired as a lonsdaleite diamond. She was pin-pricked with recurring night terrors and daily anxiety attacks undulated between multiple victims: Herself and herself and herself and herself. Every day is another betrayal. A break up north would give her the breathing space to clear her head.

She was one of the city's many ghost children – sucked in and lost to the tsunami of concrete, fox piss alley ways, and graffi-tied tiny kiosks and salons hunched together like crooked decaying teeth. Any source of nature growing in the cracks or verging along pavements were bedraggled with used condoms, piles of fly tipped sofas and broken cupboards and dirty nappies dumped by the side of roads. Just a few streets away, a man's body was found in a skip, head first with legs sticking out like candles on a birthday cake. Just like everyone else in this hellmouth, she can't afford to leave and can't afford to stay – stuck on a meagre wage that just about covers the cost of rent and bills. She lives off cheese on toast, leftover Chinese take-away and coffee.

The clouds were the colour of pewter and the moon above was a grimy coin. The weather was as sour as her mood. The scrabble of people annoyed her – rushing past and crashing into each other like sullen dodgems–a swarming canvas of travellers scurrying in flashes of colour whilst Stephanie checked timing for the next train and people watched. A buddhist monk in orange robes and nike shoes sat on a bench picking his nose then wiped it on his sleeve whilst a young mum took out her iphone to film her child having a tantrum on the damp ground, a beautiful girl with an oval face and red tresses sits crossed legged by a lamppost reading a book about vampires and a tall man wearing a monocle delighted in reading a newspaper in the rain falling through the fragments of light and ink – the headline read 'Mysterious beast from the river drowns woman', his pirate cutthroat face pensive, with one gluey blind eye, the other sparkled with dark deeds as he leaned into the shadowed wall. Stephanie brought her earpods to her ears to listen to 'The Doors' "People are strange..." She mutters along in agreement, the music drowns out the noise of the bedlam around her.

PART TWO

Wandering through the train station tuckshop, Stephanie thinks about home: the wooden floors, the mould behind the toilet she forgot to clean, the pantry cupboard brimming with packets of crisps and her collection of cups she'd stolen as souvenirs from countless cafe's. The spindly spider plant on her dusty living room window sill, crystals dotted by doorways for luck, the pack of tarot in her bedside cabinet with her romp switch, glow in the dark nipple tassles and kama sutra card game hidden under a book of erotic photography. She thought of women like herself who repressed the rainstorm inside them, who didn't know how to let it fall and form a river to form a path and flush out the ancient wound in their blood to set them free and roam in beauteous countries. She watched one woman with ebony curls scribble away in a diary and wondered if she had a rainstorm inside her too?

Settling in a seat by a window caked in dead flies, Stephanie sipped her herbal tea and scrolled through video reels, her train would arrive in 20 minutes on platform four. A woman to her left watched her like an arrowed queen, her dark eyes blink in quick succession and half close in feline laziness. Her smile– half lemon, half sugar. She was Romany, dressed in a red maxi dress with a red veil resting lightly on her long black hair. She wore a necklace charm of a woman riding a horse and she held a basket of candied pink apples. The woman smiled and offered her an apple.

'I saw your radiant pink hair and thought you'd like something just as sweet? Kooshti Loli Phabai? Lollipop?... I'm Didem by the way.'

'Stephanie. I'm not in the best mood so whatever you're

trying to sell me, I'm not interested plus I don't want to get my hands sticky on a train.'

Didem smiled wild and said 'Perhaps I can be a good distraction and lift your mood? I'm not selling anything, this caramel apple is a gift for you, might cheer you up.' and she brought the basket closer to Stephanie which was brimming with succulent caramel, toffee, honey and treacle apples on sticks. 'Go on, pick some Kooshti Lollipops, it can't hurt, I'll wrap them in a paper bag.' She bit into the delicious flesh of an apple herself, savouring the taste with each crunch. Didem's voice had a vibrant certainty that made you feel excited and safe, reeling you in to taste each word she utters.

Stephanie rolled her eyes, "Ok, fine. Thank you" and grabbed four apples, one of each flavour – she'd snack on them later. Shoving them in her satchel like a squirrel storing nuts in a tree crevice. Didem smelled of cinnamon and a soft floral fragrance – Something holy. Her olive opalescent skin glowed. There was a white lightening in her eyes. With the point of her index finger towards Stephanie she began to hum. A lullaby-like canticle.

> *Mouths wet with life, yet stabbed and staggered,*
> *so deep*
> *All the hurt that we bury and keep*
> *Four times with knives, a heart so weak*
> *The brain, the body, the cunt so meek*
> *Soil for spirit for soil, what desire we seek*
> *The rage we bury, deep in the earth*
> *Goddess of death and the birth*

The full pink moon illuminates the night,
Eat the elixir of ambrosia so light.
Of the sweet, sweet love we bite.

Enchanted for a moment, Stephanie didn't think to ask why this odd woman chose to approach her or seemed to notice her misery. But asked 'What do those words mean?' still in a daze, a rosy haze from whatever had been released in the words.

Didem adjusted her veil and said 'It's about death as a road to awe, perhaps it's a song about becoming? A song for a woman becoming beauty, setting her soul free?'

Weirded out, Stephanie grabbed her bag and tea and ran for the train that had just arrived, settled in coach D. She began flipping through a Stephen King novel before slumping into her chair, falling asleep.

PART THREE

Five hours later Stephanie steps off the train to a pale pebble sky, feathered with clouds and dusky hillsides. She is in need of a hot shower and she's hangry. She also really needed to take a shit and didn't fancy going into a public bathroom, luckily her dad pulled up in his van, Metallica echoing out the open windows. Remembering the sweet apples in her satchel she picked up one sticky delight and crunched on it carelessly. Jumping into the front seat, he asks 'How was your day?'

Stephanie shrugged and replied 'uneventful except some strange woman gave me apples.' She recalled Didem's syrupy smile telling tales of a temple by the river, of veiled women keening and drinking Salep from orchid plants during the dark moon.

Her dad replied 'It's a funny old world and you do seem to attract the weirdos, like moths to a flame.'

Finishing one apple, Stephanie reaches her delicate hands into her bag, bangles jangle as she pulls out another. Taking a moment to smell its notes of cotton candy, vanilla trills and blueberry tart tang – A siren calls from the core. The juice spurts and fizzes down her mouth as she takes a snow white bite. She is dream bitten as the taste floods her tongue. She vaguely hears her dad talk of canoeing in the lake but Stephanie is in a fever dream. The fragments of these pink apples melts into her blood. They were so moreish! An effervescent electric horizon sparkled down her throat. She had never tasted apples like this! Where were they from? Who really was Didem?

Her dad's cottage squatted by the side of the lake, hunched like a broad shouldered man fishing for trout. The shadows of the wind-blown trees scribbled inky abstract blueprints across the nearby waters and the dandelions marched across the country-side, ravenous little lions feasting on the sun. Walking up the garden path, the place smelled of dust and rosemary. The crickets chirped in the blackberry hedge and the birds, like gilded brooches pinned to the trees, sang to the watermelon sky.

In the guest room, Stephanie fell asleep. When she woke up, her body felt bendy, soft, frothy, unfamiliar. She spots a rosy stain on the bed sheet where she lay. She checked her knickers to make sure she hadn't started surfing the crimson wave, Her fingers were a vibrant pink and purple, malleable and squishy. She plucked at her index finger and her nail detaches deli-cately. Running to the bathroom, almost slipping from the fric-tion between the rug and marble floor, she stares at her reflection amongst the toothpaste, body butters and razors. She held her breath and brought her left hand to her cheek slowly. Staring into the pools of her cherry eyes, she had transformed into an amalgamation of sweets and fruit, a rainbow, sugar sweet candy woman. Bendy limbs, honeycombed heart leaking liquid gold, marshmallow breasts, jelly bean nipples, dragon fruit hips, gum drop toes, sinew made of strawberry laces, Blackpool rock bones, pomegranate plush lips.

Even in the stark bathroom light, she found herself tasty, mouth watering at the sight of her tropical body. Erasing thoughts–hungry thoughts from her head she anxiously chewed on a finger before sucking and licking it with pleasure, until it was just a stump on a palm made of liquorice. Horrified, she puked up skittles and cherries into the sink. She choked back the tears and memories that came flooding through like a sugar rush. Betrayal, heartbreak, stuck in a life she never wanted, a shitty flat she can't afford, an aching for her childhood. The pain inside grew and grew like a current dappled with caramel.

She laughed and cried and screamed and laughed some more. What is this? What the fuck is this? She thought she gave up her heart long ago to a man who was really an abyss, who ate up her soul, slurping at it like an addict, a love crayoned incubus. But her heart began to sprout leaves and oh how it expanded and ached deep and dull, how it pushed the hurt up and out of her until she coughed up starburst and lemon zest!

Holding her chest, heaving pineapple breath, Stephanie grabbed her spare key, a hoodie and satchel and ran out of the house.

PART FOUR

Texting her friend Rob as she hurries down the road

Stef: Rob I'm a fruity woman!

Rob: What the fuck Stef?

Stef: I'm a walking sweet shop!

Rob: Are you drunk?

Stef: I'm a fucking sticky toffee colourful bitch!

Rob: Yes we all know this you weirdo

Stef: No seriously, Rob I'm changing, I'm not myself

Rob: A time for whisky and making a new 'I hate myself and wanna die playlist'?

Stef: Rob, be serious. Something is happening to me...I'm yellow and pink and purple...

Rob: Yellow? Is it infected? Got TCP?

Stef: What? No! I mean, parts of me ARE banana yellow or Lemony zest

Rob: ....What have you been smoking?

Stef: I gotta go, I'm melting...

Rob: Stef, wait!..........Stef!

Stephanie wandered the cobbled streets of the little town situated between the stretch of hills. As she walked, the scent of peaches trailed behind her, making passersby stop, breathing it in with euphoria curled on their lips. Her squishy limbs became tacky and sticky against the stones.

She was melting like fruit gums in a hot mouth. She caught glimpses of herself in cafe windows set against the bewildered stares of drab people looking out at her luminous, gum drop skin like hungry ghosts sipping tea, their mini knives slicing toasted scones with an awakened desire long forgotten deep in their bellies. She went past the butcher's shop, the blade from carving bloodied beef halted in mid air, the butcher transfixed by the rainbow angel dashing across the road, love hearts and blueberries popped from her feet with every step, her sweat glittering gold icing sugar in the sultry, overripe clementine sun. Stephanie left a trail of deep warm sweetness everywhere she went, leaving the towns people starved, famished like crows wishing to pick at her flesh, yearning to taste bliss on their lips.

The sharp pain in her chest rooted into her lungs and rose up into her throat, she sat down on a bench to catch her breath. A little kid toddled over to her, snapped off a nougat toe and skipped away nibbling at a piece of her candied phalange.

Stephanie, colliding with an old gutter, limped towards the fens. Having caught and twisted her left foot, she pulled it loose and flung it from herself. Its gummy bear texture gleamed in the teeth of ravenous street cats. She was a sacrificial celestial, a yummy cherub dripping with honeycomb. Resting in a grove of trees she began to sing and her body separated, unaware a crowd of people had followed and gathered nearby.

Her right arm went first, tossed it to a librarian with ink stains on her blouse. Stephanie's legs came off, tumbling towards a man holding a Guinness and a woman selling herbs. Out from her head popped her caramel eyes that rolled out into the traffic to be pecked at by pigeons and her head was tossed into the marsh waters, the fish grazed at her brain until her abalone husked skull was washed down the river. People continued to spill out from cafes and boutiques to watch, the butcher and sweet shop owner ran out with empty jars to catch bits of Stephanie's juicy flung flesh. Her thighs slapped against lampposts, her knees whacked against a school window leaving a trail of treacle sliding down the glass. Her arse—a milky opal bloom was being lapped up in abandon by an accountant on all fours, his tongue greedily licking whipped cream. The roof of her mouth, a chapel of reddening—the way day dies as her lips were chewed by the policeman. The doctor took a scalpel to this dreamy universe, cut out her wishbone and feasted on her ovaries like chocolate eggs. The purple clouds of her body sent everyone into a lavender haze feeding frenzy. The dentist indulged at pulling out her coconut teeth, picking them like daisy petals. A swim instructor who resembled Pedro Pascal clasped her cunt like a conch— fizzing sherbet from its clit, he sucked on it, the nectar of a goddess pouring candied sand down his cherishing mouth. The rest of her began to melt in the summer rain.

All that was left was her heart cocooned by her ribcage bobbing in the marsh waters, a carcass of starbursts. Her bones, prisms of light–gleaming. Butterscotch sweet.

The beasts of the world came to perch on her beauty, to drink her tears like something consecrated–A Seraphim tasty offering!

When the crowd dispersed, disorientated by the sugar rush. A veiled woman with eyes liquid gold, trudged through the reeds, picked the heart from the ribs like an apple and placed it in her basket. She would plant it in the soil of an orchard by a nearby brooke and watch its valves split open for a sprout to break free. She will watch an apple tree grow from the heart and with each new growth Stephanie will sing a rhapsodic melody out into the velveteen sky.

This short story is symbolic for the choices many women struggle with. Remain complacent and fall in line with societal expectations and ultimately waft through life–Depressed, defeated and lost or break free and discover yourself, follow your dreams, become successful. You often see when women begin to shine— The greedy gluttons want a piece of that sweetness and the jealous bastards want to tear you apart and destroy you.

It's in the trauma that the old you and your old wounds fall away for the vampires and the ghosts to eat up–these kinds of people enjoy feasting on the suffering of others. But what's left is a brand new you, growing wild, beautiful and fruitful–A transformation–A rebirth and a realisation of your worth.

SKIN IN THE GAME

BY DEBORAH SULLIVAN BRENNAN

E ve should have known that observing Taco Tuesday on Thursday would lead to a clash with Vikings.

But she had midterms Friday morning, and nothing jump-started a study session like fish tacos. Her roommate Clara, of course, preferred carne asada.

Ordering her mahi-mahi taco plate, Eve watched her friend's eyes drift from the menu to a man. A tall, golden-skinned surfer had stacked his board against the picnic table and was devouring his meal. Clara glanced at him under her lashes, and he returned the gesture with a broad smile.

"Come on Clara, you don't have time for flirting," Eve chided her friend. "We are not even halfway through class notes."

Eve shied away from guys, knowing they would inevitably become bothersome. It was the curse of her kind. The hassles started in high school, when moon-eyed boys followed her home from school or showed up at her water polo games to gawk.

Eve wasn't the top goal-scorer, but was by far the most

aggressive defender. And she could hold her breath for an inhumanly long time, which allowed her to crush opponents in underwater brawls. She felt at ease in her skin during those games, which made it a nuisance when boys turned up to ogle her. One or two seemed nice enough that she shared her cell number. Boy, did she regret that! They texted her at all hours, sharing grandiose ambitions and terrible poetry. What about me makes them feel so smug about themselves, she wondered?

Her mom Riona had been married three times, the last to Eve's father. That marriage ended when Eve was six; she had not seen her dad since. Women in her family drew attention from men, but once they did they couldn't escape it; her mom had to change cities to evade controlling husbands. More than a decade ago she Riona moved with her young daughter from Galway to Oceanside, hoping for a clean break. It was tough leaving their extended family in Ireland, but even there Eve had never truly fit. Her dark hair and hazel eyes - mossy brown, swirled with green - stood out from her blonde and ginger cousins.

Riona moved them into a small, shabby apartment near the harbor, but Eve was just happy to smell salt spray on her walk to school. Home wasn't inside anyway; it was in the water.

Eve met Clara her freshman year at Oceanside High. She was the first girl to make Eve feel welcome in California, although neither knew at first how much they had in common. They didn't fit into the mainstream high school crowd, but Clara embraced her outsider status, wearing Doc Martens and leather miniskirts, and sneaking out to a tattoo parlor to get a wolf inked on her arm. The goth girl personna didn't get her elected to student government or chosen for the cheer squad, but it got her noticed.

Eve, by contrast, aimed to blend in, although she never quite managed. When she wasn't in a swimsuit her uniform was a beachy mix of gauze skirts and tank tops, paired with crocheted ponchos. The goal was California girl cool, but the final look, she acknowledged, was hippie throwback. Clara used to tease her: "Woodstock called; it wants its clothes back."

"At least it's more comfortable than head-to-toe animal hide," Eve retorted.

Clara smirked: "You have no idea."

Eve worked to suppress her soft Irish brogue, but still looked and sounded different to classmates. If you only knew, she thought later! It's not just the accent, it's the fins and whiskers.

Their transformations began around junior year of high school. Clara's parents had prepared her for what would happen when her wolf features emerged, but Eve's mom merely hinted at what it meant to be a selkie. When her limbs began to stretch and change one day as she swam out far past Oceanside pier into open water, she panicked.

"Mom there's something wrong with me," she blurted out at home.

"There's nothing wrong," her mom reassured. "I'll show you."

They hopped in their old Honda Civic and parked along the Coastal Highway. Riona waded in and beckoned her daughter to follow.

Riona's dark hair rippled in the waves, spreading across her body in a dense pelt. Bristles sprouted on her cheeks as she nodded to her daughter. Eve was so transfixed by her mothers' transformation, she didn't immediately notice her own limbs turn to flippers. The seal form took over, plunging Eve into the surf, as her human consciousness receded.

She glided among the currents and dove deeper than even her exceptional swimming ability allowed in human form.

Encountering some sea bass, she snapped one up and devoured it in three bites.

Gulping down the last bite of a perfectly crispy mahi-mahi taco near UC San Diego years later, she considered how raw fish tastes even better.

"Why don't you try dating a lycanthrope?" Clara suggested. "He would understand your abilities better than a human guy. I could introduce you."

"How would that work? What would our children be? Wolfies? Selkanthropes?"

"You have to think of it as an intercultural relationship, like you're Irish, he's American."

Eve paused a moment before blurting out something she might regret. Clara was her college roommate, her high school bestie, and the only friend who understood her for who she really was.

What Clara didn't understand was Eve's life of flight and fear, constantly escaping her mom's obsessive admirers or ex-husbands. Selkie women sometimes mated with human men, but the pairings usually ended in manipulation and control.

Celtic lore tells of a fisherman who discovered a beautiful woman naked on the seashore and fell instantly in love with her. He found her sealskin stashed in nearby rocks and hid it in his attic, compelling her to marry him. For years she remained a dutiful wife, bearing him several children, until she discovered his hiding place, reclaimed her skin and returned to the sea.

It was a poignant fairytale, but for Eve, it was her family history. Riona had escaped that calamity several times, eluding men whose love turned to obsession. Eve planned to avoid it altogether.

By contrast, Clara's mom and dad were bonded more tightly than any couple she knew; lifetime matings were the norm for wolves and their shape-shifting counterparts. Eve envied her friend's close-knit family, stable parents and protective older brother. Yes, they were lycanthropes, with the secrecy and danger that entailed. But they bore it together.

"Clara, your family is different," Eve said, measuring her words. "You're born to bond for life. I was raised to avoid that."

Thursday night they reviewed class notes, highlighted key textbook passages and wrote an outline and study guide. Or, to be precise, Eve did. Clara popped in her earbuds to scroll TikTok for party listings and watched videos of the Swedish doom metal band "Ghost," also known as the bastard lovechild of Black Sabbath and Abba.

"Seriously, Clara, you have to help," Eve said. "I'm doing all the work."

"Your job is studying," Clara explained patiently. "My job is finding parties."

"I like bonfires," Eve said. "You take us to dumpster fires."

"Also called raves," Clara noted. "But this weekend we're going to the Vista Viking Fest. There's a lycanthrope afterparty at one of the camps."

"Nooo, I told you: no wolf boys."

"They'll have mead there!"

Eve conceded: "I suppose so."

Their midterms went fine. Eve was sure she earned A's in English literature and biology, and Clara would probably pull B's, thanks to her help.

That evening they dressed to go out. Eve pulled on a long, plum-colored skirt with a drapey wrap.

"Eve, no," Clara exclaimed when she emerged. "Stevie Nicks called, she wants..."

"I know, she wants her clothes back," Eve snapped.

"No, Stevie told me to burn them. But I can fix this."

Clara was already in costume - a black and silver corset with a ruched skirt and high black boots. She rustled around her closet and pulled out a green linen gown trimmed in gold embroidery. Eve pulled it on, grudgingly admitting it did look more period-appropriate than her usual Woodstock-wear. Clara pushed her down onto an armchair with the gentle force generally used to groom a cat, and applied smoky eyeliner and nude lip gloss.

"Now that I'm done de-embarassing you, we can call an Uber," Clara said, standing back to admire her work.

They arrived at the festival and slipped through a back entry. A big, cranky-looking bouncer (definitely a lycanthrope, Eve decided,) glared at them until Clara pulled up a code on her cellphone. He nodded and waved them into a canvas tent. Fellow festival-goers were dressed in suede tunics, with fur capes and hoods. Some had pointed horns protruding from their heads; Eve pondered whether they were decorative head-gear or real appendages.

Clara had explained there would be lycanthropes and likely other shape-shifters there, so you never know what you might get. Be friendly. Be careful. Don't be drunk.

Eve grabbed a bottle of cider from a bucket as she walked in. She didn't plan to get hammered, but she wasn't going to get through the night sober.

Two lycanthropic boys a couple years younger than her were sucking nitrous from whipped cream canisters. With each hit their features sharpened and distorted, their faces grew hairier, then snapped back to normal. After particularly deep hits one of the boys doubled over laughing. On closer inspection Eve saw that his friend's face had mostly resumed human shape. Mostly, except for one craggy brow bone that jutted out distinctly, with a crown of bristly hairs poking from it.

"What? What's so funny," he asked his friend, who was incapacitated by a fit of giggles.

Eve snickered too at this weird version of teen mischief.

Harmless, she thought. Stupid, but harmless. She wandered through the crowd, stopping to listen to a pirate thrash band playing metal versions of sea shanties.

"Eve look," Clara whispered. "It's the guy from the taco stand."

The bronzed surfer was sitting on a barstool, wearing a dark red linen tunic. He's kind of cute, Eve thought, before he glanced over at them.

"Eve, I hate to admit this because I spotted him first, but he's looking at you," Clara nudged her.

The surfer set down his empty mug and approached them.

"I'm Shane," he said, extending his hand.

"This is my friend Eve," Clara announced. "I'm Clara. Ooh, I need to fix my contacts. I'll be right back."

She doesn't wear contacts, Eve thought. Lame. But she had to admit, this guy was hot: tan skin, amber eyes, wavy brown hair. Turned out Shane had a pretty good sense of humor. He was studying engineering, so clearly not as dumb as the whip cream boys.

"Do you like him?" Clara asked excitedly, pulling her friend aside. "I asked around. He's from an old San Diego clan. I should warn you though, some of his family members aren't as open-minded as the rest of us."

Over the years, Eve had learned about the factions within lycanthrope culture. Most sought balance with their human counterparts and other shape-shifters. But a handful, including some powerful, old families, sought to dominate other beings. Eve had a few uncomfortable brushes with that crowd on some of her outings with Clara. She didn't care to repeat those encounters.

"No way," Eve shook her head. She had enough trouble with human men, let alone xenophobic werewolves.

"He's not like them," Clara continued. "Hear me out. His

friends told me he supports tolerance and diversity. You should give him a chance."

Shane found them chatting beside a mead cask and placed his hand on Eve's shoulder. It tingled, she thought, perplexed by the pleasant sensation.

"Can I borrow your friend," he asked Clara.

"All yours!" Clara said, trotting off towards the bar.

"I know you're a selkie," he said.

Great, Eve thought, flushing. Clara dragged me here and now she's outed me.

"It's your eyes," he said. "I've met a few of your kind and your eyes are always...otherworldly."

He tilted her chin up, compelling her to look at him.

"So I thought maybe we could..."

Eve started to pull away.

"Go to a bonfire?" he asked. "I thought the beach might be more your speed."

"Uh, I guess so," Eve answered, silently lamenting the long, heavy gown that Clara had dressed her in.

"We could swing by your place if you need to change?" he suggested.

Shane sped along the Coastal Highway in his midnight blue Mustang and pulled up at her apartment near UC San Diego. Eve opened the door, relieved she'd had the presence of mind to tidy up before she left. Shane waited in the small kitchen while she stepped into her room, shimmied out of her Viking garb and into a bikini. She pulled on her comfy cotton skirt, glad that Clara hadn't burned it as threatened.

She reached onto the top shelf of her closet as she always did, and checked to make sure it was safe: her seal skin. This was her lifeline, the thing that made her both more and less than human. On a whim, she grabbed the skin, popped it in her bag and returned to Shane.

They walked down to La Jolla Shores, where a few of Shane's friends were gathered around a bonfire, sharing a cooler of beers. The red tide had arrived, as it did every couple years. Algae stained the sea rusty red during daylight and exploded in blue flashes of bioluminescence by night.

Shane sprinted into the surf. Eve followed, hiking her skirt around her hips and exposing long, muscular legs. Shane looked at her with something like hunger as she waded into the sea, neon blue phytoplankton shimmering around her. She had seen the look before, but never returned it. So she was surprised to realize that she kind of wanted a bite of him, too.

Instead she reached into the surf, splashed him and ran toward shore.

He chased her to the waterline and caught her hand.

"Do it," he said. "Change, now. I want to see you..."

Eve hadn't intended to comply, but she slipped into her skin and felt her limbs stretching, her pelt sprouting. Shane's face shifted too; his sculpted cheekbones sharpened, fur appeared and eyes brightened from amber to gold.

Shane pulled her closer and pressed his lips to hers, as they sunk into the sand. He tasted like raspberries and gold, with a trace of something darker. Blood? Eve set the thought aside and nestled closer, savoring her first real kiss. Of course she did not count the sloppy makeout sessions with some high school dates. This was different, more of a dance than those early stumbles. The well-honed caution beacon in her mind sent up its customary warning flare. But the part of her mind directing her to crawl into his lap shot it down.

Their embrace continued for what seemed an infinity, but must have been minutes. His friends had doused the bonfire and left. Shane drove her home and kissed her again outside the door, and again in the entryway and in the small living room. Eve set her bag down by the couch and curled into his arms.

After about a half hour, Shane untwined from her embrace and rose to leave.

"I should go," he said softly, sounding very much like he did not like his own suggestion.

Clara arrived home minutes later, sparkling with curiosity.

"Tell me," she insisted.

"Let me get my jammies on," Eve answered, realizing she was still sea-soaked. She slid out of her damp clothes and swimsuit and into pajamas, then reached into her tote to put her skin back in its hiding place.

It was gone.

Her sealskin was missing. All the terror and panic of her childhood bubbled to the surface.

Eve didn't hear herself scream when Clara came running in.

"What's wrong?" Clara demanded, knowing but not wanting to believe the worst.

"He took it," Eve sobbed. "That bastard!"

"I'm so sorry," Clara said, panicked. "I wanted you to be happy."

"I was fine," Eve cried. "Now I'm nothing."

She had to talk to her mother. Riona had been through this before. But her captors were human. How could Eve reclaim her skin from a lycanthrope? She was about to call her mom when her cellphone rang. Shane.

"I wasn't going to keep it," he insisted in a choked voice. "My dad wanted to see it, you know, to check things out."

"Where is it?" Eve demanded, her voice flat but deadly.

She heard a scuffle and another voice came on the phone, older and harsher.

"Fish-eater," the man spat. "You're nothing. We own you!"

Idiot! Eve thought. You took my skin, but I won't let you keep yours.

"Come on, let's find your mom," Clara said.

When they arrived at her apartment in Oceanside, Riona instantly knew something was wrong, and a split second later knew what it was. She threw her arms around her daughter.

"This is why I left Ireland: to keep you safe," she said as Eve wept.

"We're never going to be safe," Eve sobbed.

Clara was fidgeting on her phone and announced, "I've got the address."

They zoomed in on Google Earth to an old ranch in Fallbrook. Horse pastures and goat pens were ringed by dense, overgrown avocado orchards. Really overgrown: these trees were a fairytale forest of gnarled branches and dense canopy.

Forty minutes later they parked on the edge of a winding fire road and then hiked through the grove. Finally, the trees thinned and opened onto a wide lawn, where brick walkways wove around sparkling fountains. A tall house loomed above it framed in dark wood beams and walls of river rock. It radiated money and power.

"We should go around back," Clara said, zooming in on the Google Earth image to reveal a rear servant's door.

They slipped behind the house toward the entry, passing a large pool lined in blue mosaic tiles, and a smaller pond dotted with rocks and lily pads, and flashing with koi.

Clara approached the door first and jiggled the handle. She was trying to pry it open when it burst open and two men emerged, charging toward them. One was huge, bald and black-clad; your typical bone-crushing bodyguard. The other was lanky, with ginger hair and a furtive look.

Eve blurted out the first thing that came to mind: "Is Shane home?"

"Yes, and he's expecting you," the bald gargoyle snapped.

An instant later he began to change, his neck thickening,

shoulders broadening and snout lengthening as he grew at least a foot taller, sprouting wiry fur. His companion shifted too, into a tawny, slinking form of canid.

"A coyotal," Clara whispered loudly.

Other canid shape-shifters sometimes associated with lycanthropes, but they were almost always subordinate to the apex predators. He's not the top dog here, Eve realized.

She made for the safest place she saw: the water. With the coyotal guard on her heels, she dove into the koi pond and plunged underwater. Even without her skin, she could hold her breath several minutes and out-swim just about anyone. Looking up through the lotus, she saw her pursuer dog-padding towards her. Coyotes are poor swimmers, she remembered. He's out of his element.

The guard sloshed forward, scanning the water to find his prey. Eve grabbed him by the fur and tugged. His face plunged under and he reached for her hair, yanking hard. Rage and pain released a burst of adrenaline as Eve pulled him under, clasping at his throat. This was her superpower: underwater scuffles. She had spent years bashing other girls in water polo in preparation for this moment. She pushed harder, knocking his head against the wall of the pond.

The coyotal guard thrashed and coughed; clearly he was inhaling water. Good. She could stay submerged minutes longer, but this trash-dog couldn't, and his flailing would only make him succumb sooner.

He went out quickly. Eve let go as his eyes rolled closed and he dropped to the pond bottom. She hauled herself out of the water and scanned the scene.

Clara was facing down the lycanthrope thug. Eve had seen her friend change many times, and would have assumed she had no chance against that hulking wolf. Clara was pretty, even cuddly, when transformed, with silver fur and yellow eyes.

But there was nothing endearing about her now.

Clara's golden eyes blazed radioactive. She was fierce and fast, snapping at the heels of her much larger attacker. Eve watched him reach down and swat at her friend, knocking Clara halfway across the patio, her face skidded on the pavers.

Blood dripped from her muzzle. Clara raced back, whipping around him, howling. This time he couldn't reach her, and as he bent to strike her, Eve saw his legs buckle, blood soak his calves. Clara had hamstrung him. She retreated, gloating, his blood mingling with hers on her snout.

Where was Riona? Eve scanned in a panic for her mom. If they had taken her own sealskin, would they also kidnap her mother? A second later, she saw her explode from the water.

Riona torpedoed from the pool in seal form, rammed the injured werewolf and toppled him underwater. She jumped up in a triumphant flip and dove atop him, clamping onto the scruff of his neck with her locking jaws and driving him to the bottom.

Clara sat on a deck chair licking her wounds. Riona emerged from the pool, dripping. With both guards dispatched, they pondered their next steps for finding Eve's sealskin.

"Where would a rich, cocky bastard keep something valuable?" Riona mused.

It occurred to the three of them at once: "His gun safe."

As they huddled to form a plan, Eve noticed that the coyotal had hauled himself out of the koi pond, and was puking up swamp water into the plants beside it. The lycanthrope guard had also somehow survived drowning and was lying on the pool steps panting heavily.

"We better move while they're still out of commission," Riona said.

Eve sensed movement behind her, and felt a heavy hand on her shoulder. She whipped around to see Shane grinning at her, as if he had just left her apartment after their date. What was he thinking? Did he forget he had ruined her life?

"Eve, you're so beautiful," he gushed.

I doubt it, she thought. Her clothes were torn and she was covered in pond sludge. She was pretty sure the coyotal had ripped out a chunk of her hair.

"I have a gift for you," Shane continued. "I know you love seafood."

He was carrying a bucket of something orange and slimy. His koi fish!

"Shane, I don't eat Koi. No one does... except coyotes." She noticed the coyotal guard swatting a paw into the pool, forgetting entirely about the battle that just ensued as he clumsily fished for a snack. "Put those fish back."

"But I want you to be happy," he said with a crooked smile that signaled, "selkie crush" and also, "half-changed lycanthrope."

She looked at him closely. Upon closer inspection his amber eyes appeared just... brown. His golden skin had an orange cast below his patches of fur. Ew, a spray tan. Suddenly he looked less Viking god and more Baywatch knockoff.

"You know what would make me happy?" she said with false coquetry. "Show me your gun safe."

"Okay, sure," he said, trotting toward the house.

He is more like the whip-cream suckers than I thought, Eve realized. So easily manipulated! She followed him into his home.

The front door led directly to a spacious room with a vaulted ceiling braced by thick wood beams. Circular shields in shades of red, black and blue hung on the walls, with Norse helmets of engraved bronze.

"A Viking long hall," Clara whispered. "They must have shipped in these artifacts. This would cost a fortune!"

Shane led them through the great hall, into an adjacent room lined in wall-to-wall bookshelves stacked with leather-bound tomes.

"My dad collects these," Shane told Eve. "They're really old."

He plucked one off the shelf and opened it, revealing illuminated lettering and vivid illustrations on fragile parchment.

"Careful," Riona admonished, gently closing the book and sliding it back on the shelf. "And your gun safe?"

"Oh, right," Shane laughed, just remembering why he brought them into the library.

He opened an ancient, carved wooden door to reveal a perfectly modern black vault. Shane punched a series of numbers on the keypad and the safe door swung open.

The size of a closet, the safe housed more than a dozen firearms, from Browning hunting rifles to vintage Italian rosewood shotguns. There were also curved battle-axes, steel blades and a crossbow.

"Quite an armory you've got," Clara said, stroking the polished stock of an Italian gun.

"Yeah, my dad collects these too!" Shane bragged.

"What else does he collect?" Eve pressed, eager to get back on track. "Do you have any exotic animal fur?"

"Oh yeah, in the back," Shane said helpfully.

She rifled through the closet, feeling for the smooth pelt of her sealskin. Her hand touched a cool, metal object. Curious, she pulled out an intricately etched replica of Thor's hammer, Mjölnir. Eve set it on the ground and reached around the firearms until she found the length of thick, glossy fur. She clasped it under her arm and turned toward the door.

"I'll just take this and go now, shall I?" she said with forced nonchalance.

"Okay," he agreed. "I'll come with you."

Eve stared at her mom in panic. Shane tagging along with them was not part of the plan.

"You have to put these things back," Rionna said smoothly. "Then you can come later."

Eve was impressed at how persuasive her mom was. Her words were honey-coated, but carried the weight of a command. Shane hopped to it, stacking the rifles and other weapons back in the vault.

"Put everything back," someone growled behind them. "All of it!"

A man stood blocking the doorway, glowering. He was as tall as Shane - well over six feet - and half again as wide, with broad, muscled shoulders and thinning blond hair over a stony face.

"Books and weapons aren't the only thing I collect," Shane's dad snarled. "Put the sealskin back. Then you can leave with your human skin intact."

A shadow darkened his face, and crept down his body as he swelled into wolf form. Coarse hairs spread across his brow, sharpening cheekbones and bulging arms.

Clara changed then too, snapping into the lithe, agile predator that had fought the guards. The massive wolf laughed contemptuously.

"You're a pup!" he barked.

He loomed over her, pulsing with menace.

"You disappoint me, mingling with mermaids," he spat the last word as if it were an obscenity.

"Selkies," Eve corrected under her breath.

"Lycanthropes are leaders," he said, stalking around Clara, who was crouched and growling softly. "Chieftains. Rulers. Not side-kicks to sea-nymphs."

"You!" he thrust his face inches from his son's face. "You were ordered to dominate the selkie, not fall for her."

Shane was also changed, Eve noticed then, but appeared softer, rounder; a puppy, not a predator. His eyes shifted away his father, and she heard him whimpering. Incongruously, her mind drifted to wildlife videos of wolf pack structure.

His father scanned the group with derision. Then, fast as a bullet, he lunged toward Eve, grasping at the sealskin clutched in her hands. They wrestled over the skin. Shane's dad's eyes reddened with the struggle, and Eve surprised herself with the force of her grip.

Out of the corner of her eye, Eve saw her mother stand up and approach the towering creature.

"Let's see if we can all calm down now," she purred.

Shane's dad loosened his grip for a second, distracted, then tugged again. But his eyes drifted back to Riona.

Time had not diminished Riona's beauty. Her hair was still dark and shiny, a selkie perk that Eve tallied in her mental notebook. Years of swimming in the cold Pacific had left Riona slim and fit. As Eve observed this, she realized her mother was subtly changing, allowing the wildness of her seal form to enhance her human features.

Conversely, the hulking lycanthrope appeared to shrink in her presence, diminishing until he was just another grinning man, subdued by the selkie enchantment.

He dropped the sealskin, turned his full attention to Riona and held out his hand to shake hers.

"Nice to meet you," he said. "What brings you here?"

"We were just in the neighborhood," she said with a radiant smile.

Eve was astounded. What seemed destined to become a violent confrontation had suddenly turned into a creepy flirtation. Shane and his father lost all awareness that they had just stolen her skin, or that the women had broken into his home to reclaim it. Obliviously, the elder lycanthrope chit-chatted with

Riona, sharing what he presumed to be impressive facts about himself.

"I'm Niles Larson," he said, holding Riona's hand for an awkwardly long time.

The name rang a bell with Eve. Where did she know it from? Then the newspaper photos and headlines flashed back to her.

"He's that venture capitalist who's always getting sued for hostile takeovers," she whispered to Clara. "I didn't know he was one of you!"

Clara shrugged: "Tons of corporate raiders are lycanthropes. Remember 'The Wolf of Wall Street? That's not a metaphor."

Niles was gazing starstruck at Riona, gushing with cheesy pickup lines.

"Did I tell you I'm divorced," he said, with what he must have thought was a winsome smile, but looked more like indigestion. "I drive a BMW."

Eve was so engrossed in watching her mom work her spell that she failed to notice Shane fawning over her. At some point she turned back to him with annoyance when he began playing with her hair, muttering "pretty."

"Stop it," she swatted his hand away.

"Okay, time to go," Riona announced.

"So soon?" Niles said. "I want to show you my golf trophies."

"How about next time?" she suggested.

"Okay, sounds good," he acquiesced.

Eve tucked her sealskin into her bag and began to shut the door to the safe. It wouldn't do for them to find it wide open when they came to their senses. She looked at the Mjölnir replica, and in a fit of kleptomania, snatched it up and dropped it in the bag as well.

"I'll just take this too, all right?" she said to Shane.

"Sure, anything you want," he nodded happily.

The two men walked them out, back through the hall, with Niles stopping to point out portraits of himself with various politicians and pro athletes at different fund-raisers and sports events.

"Here's me with Tiger Woods," Shane's dad bragged.

"He's a tigrid," Clara giggled. "His fangs popped out at the PGA tournament!"

Niles insisted on driving them to their car in a golf cart, with Riona in front and the three students crammed in the backseat. He grabbed some avocados off a tree and thrust them in Riona's hands.

"Here, take some avocados, you can make some guacamole!" he said, pressing the fruit tenderly into Riona's hands.

"Bye bye," he waved fondly as they drove off.

"What just happened?" Eve demanded of her mom.

"This is how it starts," Riona said bluntly. "Infatuation, obsession, then domination."

"Won't they follow us?" she asked, worried. "Won't they find us?"

"No, not now. They're in the charmed phase; they'll forget as soon as we leave."

Eve considered that as they drove along the Coastal Highway, where the first light of dawn illuminated the waves, turning the page on their surreal night. Selkies possessed some allure that drew men toward them but eventually consumed them. Until that point it was as if it never happened.

When they returned home, Clara staggered into her room and collapsed face-down on her bed.

Eve poked around the apartment, mindful of the two precious objects she had to safeguard.

Where to put Mjölnir? She set it on a bookshelf, but then reconsidered; too conspicuous. She walked into the small kitchen, opened a cabinet with a few pieces of cookware, and set Thor's hammer next to her crab pot. This will come in handy for cracking shellfish, Eve thought with satisfaction.

Now, about her sealskin. She knew she needed a more secure place to hide it than the top shelf she had stashed it on for the past year or so. A drawer would be hidden, but obvious. Her suitcase? Not safe enough. She browsed through her closet, then pulled out her wetsuit. Eve slipped the sealskin in and watched it mold to the inner contours of the neoprene, fusing her selkie nature to her human life.

STALK

BY CHRISTOPHER PENDER

G ermany's countryside in mid-October, in its diffuse sunlight, bathing the mountain sides, trees, flowerbeds, and trestles in its almost supernatural glow moved Julius to concede that until now he had not found a truer beauty. He sat in his train carriage that evening as the sun drew in, thanking god for the view and wishing that the moment would never end. The countenance of flawless landscape was made all that more profound by the realisation that man is the only earthly creature who is capable of appreciating it all and had it not been for his existence the meaning of all of this would have been lost.

The vibration of the train and the satisfying lullaby of its repetitive chuffing produced a feeling of blissful comfort. It was an old carriage but well kept. Along the interior, wooden panels were held in a place by rusted red iron bolts. Old but quaint embroidered curtains were neatly tied in on each side of the carriage windows. The wooden floor was worn, the surface layer eroded by many a foot fall over the years. And by each window an oil lamp sat in its niche. One was near the window on Julius' right side. It was a small carriage, empty now as the passengers had gotten off at various intervals. But there were no more stops now along the way to Bremen.

Julius would be travelling through the night reaching his destination in the morning. A new City, a new life, a new start. In this circumstance he was perfectly happy to have the time to himself. Once it became dark, he would light the lamp and read his newly enquired book, Dracula by Bram Stoker. He had only just purchased it this morning in a quaint little bookshop in Cologne. The shop interior walls were constructed of tall stacks of books. A charming idea. But he had wondered what would have happened if he had fancied a book lodged in one of the wall's foundations. Everything was dusty, even the old man whom he had purchased the book from. It was a fine place to purchase such a book Julius thought, in keeping with the mood of the genre. He remembered as he handed the money over how he had brushed the knife edge of his hand against the freshly ink pressed front page of a newspaper. "Another woman murdered by the Dresden ripper." The killer's new nickname was coined without creativity, crass. There were six victims now, in the last six months. All the more reason to get out of Dresden he thought.

The light was now dim enough as not to allow him to read by the daylight but still too bright for the lamp. He stared out the carriage window into the twilight resting his head on the seat headrest. The train had entered agrarian country now. Vast flat fields of corn, the breadbasket of Germany where men toiled, women baked large loaves of barn bread to maintain the brawn their hard-working men and the children played in the vast expanse of tall stalks until the sun turned in.

As the carriage sped along, he stared out into the mesmerizingly tall continuous wall of corn. Suddenly he glimpsed a face, yes, just one moment between two blinks of the eye and then it was gone. It was an unexpected and startling spectacle. But the features were all well accounted for in Julius's mind. It was a dog's head, with a wet glistening nose at the end of a long snout, and short, broad pointy ears. A wolf yes, there are wolves in the German wilderness. However, to Julius, even in that brief glimpse, it had two anomalous features. Firstly, although he saw the head alone it seemed to be at rather an unusual height off the ground, even more than the height of a man. And the other exotic vista were its eyes. Those eyes, they were like the eyes of a man, large hazel eyes. Julius had been shaken by the startling vision. He looked around for reassurance before remembering that he was alone in the carriage. He straightened himself on the seat, arching his back "did anyone?... no." He gulped with unease and cleared his dry throat. As if trying to depart from that moment symbolically he stood up as much as headroom would permit and then sat back down resettling into his seat. He trusted that his perception was correct but convinced himself that what he had seen had passed by altogether much too quickly to observe with due certainty. His self-dialogue, his internal reasoning began to produce a dividend.

It was now on the edge of night and Julius wasted no time in lighting his lamp. Its light reflected in the window glass pane from which he could also see his faint mirror image staring back at him. As he stared into his reflection, a briar twig tapped against the window, momentarily surprising him and in doing so revealed that he was still unsettled from the incident. He quickly drew in the curtains, drawing a boundary beyond which he would no longer be alarmed. He contemplated beginning his book, if he still currently had the constitution for it under the present developments.

Due to his unsettling encounter, he no longer wished for the extended opportunity to rest and read which had seemed so welcoming in the daylight hours. He decided to sleep. Although already wearing his coat he imitated wrapping himself with it, pulling the collar up until it touched his ears. He settled back in his seat, folding his arms and closing his eyes. He thought about summer in Dresden, he thought about the tall buildings and busy streets. He thought about the warm rays of the sun and the cafes and bookshops and the beautiful girls, all the beautiful girls. And he thought of the light of the full moon as it bathes the city in its most magnificent glow. He let himself drift away. Although his eyes were closed, he experienced an inner visual carte du jour from his many hours of observation. Mountains, flowers, razed stone granite walls, hills and pastures, tall grass, tall wheat, that face, that wolf, that man, running now, broad, and powerful, hungry, full of lust and rage, running in the darkness, eyes ablaze.

Julius opened his eyes wide. He felt a presence, an invisible presence next to him, almost imposing itself upon him. He turned his head towards the window and stared at the curtain. He looked on in trepidation. Slowly and hesitantly, he reached out and pulled back the curtain. Transposed over his reflection in the pane were those blazing eyes gazing back and him, the eyes of a wolf. But this time he was not afraid. He remembered now. In the moonlight he knew again. He bathed in the cold glow of the now visible waxing crescent of the moon, mother moon. "Some things you cannot leave behind," he thought, "no matter how much you want it."

THE SUMMER OF SLIGHT ACQUAINTANCES

BY NEEPA SARKAR

"It is a strange chilly summer this year," thought Akashi as she boarded the bus on a late June evening from Bangalore. There had been a last-minute change of plans, as Subodh, her twin brother, who was to travel with her decided to join his fiancée Juana earlier and had taken a flight to Coimbatore. Juana's family and friends had flown in from Santa Fe, Mexico to Coimbatore for the summer wedding. Choosing Coimbatore as a wedding destination appeared puerile to Akashi. She had hoped for Chennai, where she and Subodh had spent their childhood years and where she had fallen in love with Ruben, who was a teaching assistant at IIT Madras. She had fond memories of their rendezvous dotting the cityscape of Chennai, from ten years back. They were in a long-distance relationship as both had moved countries for their careers.

"Now," thought Akashi, "I can barely remember his smile and the way he looked at me." Nevertheless, they were still together more as friends than lovers though he was not anymore, the first person she called if she felt disturbed or excited.

Although twins, Subodh and Akashi, had completely different personalities and even their appearance did not match once they touched adulthood. A decade had passed by and Akashi had lost the initial sadness of not being alike to her womb companion. Graduating from MIT with a degree in Biological Engineering, Subodh had taken up an attractive job offer in a leading company based in New York. It was here that he had met Juana, a sprightly and gorgeous Mexican woman who worked in the Finance division.

Akashi smiled as she recollected what Subodh had told her eight years back as he was introduced to Juana, "I have never seen such exquisite eyes; they reveal more about me than her!" he had blurted over the phone.

Suddenly, she heard a voice, "Madam! Ticket!" Akashi, in her reverie, had walked towards the sleeper bus in the bus bay without realizing it. She pulled out her phone and showed the e-ticket to the bus driver who was busily loading the passenger baggage onto the side luggage compartment. She gave a hand to the driver and pushed her bag in. Locating her travel seat, she laid down and closed the curtains around her, preparing to spend the eight hours of her journey, mostly sleeping.

For the last five years, Akashi had spent her summers in the department of Biological Anthropology at Harvard, writing her doctoral thesis and was on the verge of completion. She was glad to get this small respite, thanks to Subodh's wedding plans. Also, she needed to verify some data from a village, near Coimbatore, for her supervisor and she had plans to get on with it once the wedding festivities were over. At 9 pm the bus started, and she called Subodh to inform and talk to her parents who were with him. She had had a light dinner from one of those budget hotels near the bus stand and as the bus picked up pace, she found herself gently soothed into an oblivion.

The bus was not quite crowded and there was a comfortable silence in the dimly lit air-conditioned interiors, lulling the passengers into a sort of languid tranquillity. It was almost midnight, the route had become immersed in fog and Akashi woke up with a start as the bus came to a sudden halt. She had travelled on this route many times, and realized that they were near the Bandipur Reserve Forest. The driver was excitedly shouting 'irunda mrgam'[1]. Akashi on her field trips and surveys to this state had picked up enough Tamil to realize that the driver must have spotted some animal crossing the road. (It was not an unusual occurrence on that road stretch). However, a sudden loud thud on top of the bus, saw the driver and conductor exchanging perplexed looks. The conductor stepped out to investigate and after several moments of silence, the stillness and calm obscurity of the night was pierced with loud shrieks of the man. Akashi ran to the front of the bus to see what the matter was, when the driver wildly gestured to her to close the bus door. He had seen the conductor being flung to the other side of the road and that had scared him out of his wits. However, he knew if the man had to be saved, he must take the bus to the other side and locate him. Before Akashi could properly shut the door, the driver hurried to take a turn. Almost everyone inside the bus was awake and a few whimpering sounds could be heard from the back seats. While taking a turn, a startled deer jumped across the road, making the driver lose control and hit a tree on the side. Akashi could barely manage to hold on to the door handle as she found herself being flung away. The last thing she remembered as she fell unconscious – a pair of big red, fuming eyes that penetrated her soul!

Screams... shouts... rustling sounds... Akashi could feel herself being dragged away by something strong. Falling in and out of consciousness, a strange fear and confusion overwhelmed her. In her brief moments of consciousness all she could see was a dense fog that kept following and engulfing her. Perhaps it was thirty seconds or it was half an hour, she had no idea. Time seemed long, dark and threatening. She had heard some yells, footsteps and shuffling sounds and that gave her hope that someone was trying to rescue her. Whenever the fog thinned a bit, she could see that it was pitch dark. The darkness was only shattered by her loud breathing and a strange scent seemed to fill up the air. She wanted to run away, but being in a dark space, she had no idea which way to run. After a few moments of being dragged, she was flung onto a grassy patch of land. She waited, trying to adjust her eyes to the darkness. A cool breeze and a soft gurgling sound made her realize that she was near a water body, probably a lake.

Akashi, mentally kept counting her heartbeats, trying to calm herself in this state of fear, alarm and confusion. If it was a wild animal that had taken her away, then why was she still alive? Where was it now? Was she really going to die? Questions thronged her mind relentlessly as fear raged inside her. She knew she had to keep waiting till daybreak to get any kind of help- that is- if she was alive till that time!

Jihan watched her from afar, he wanted to kill her and all the passengers on that bus, and for that matter, whoever he could lay his hands on! He had been doing this routine of murder for the past six years! One fateful night, after killing most of the men of his village, he had run in his blood-soaked clothes to this forest. Sambhu Sardar, a large man and the leader, along with his notorious local criminal gang, had witnessed the whole episode of Jihan's transition into a furious and livid beast who could only dwell in destruction and fury. He saw Jihan running towards them in his bloodied clothes, his madness on the verge of ebbing, then Sambhu had jumped in front and fought with him. "I want this beast," he thought, "this beast that can run amok and cause infinite fear." Rendering Jihan unconscious with a blow to the back of his neck, Sambhu had carried him to his lair. There, Jihan woke up, three days later, and saw the relief in one of Sambhu's remaining eyes, the other, long since destroyed in a tiger attack! Nowhere to go, no one to look for, Jihan decided to stay with Sambhu and his gang. He knew there was no salvation for him and his life path now could only lead him to further annihilation and ruin.

Six years had passed by since that night and no one, now, called him Jihan anymore, he was 'Mrgam' – the beast who prowled in the forest causing death to many! He felt no pain. No one recognised him in his village anymore. He had left his home the night the village men had ravaged his Kaaveri and killed her because she was found studying near the Brahmin temple on the edge of the lake. Jihan had grown up in this caste-based, hierarchical village but had assumed that that's how things were and always would be.

He had a sharp mind and since that year when some social activists from Chennai came to the village and convinced his parents to admit him in the village government school, there was no looking back for him. Aneesh Babu, the teacher in school, encouraged him throughout and guided him to complete his engineering. "Education is all you have, Jihan, and it will never disappoint you!" Aneesh Babu would often remind him.

Now, Jihan barely remembered his father's face. Sometimes, memories of his father's soothing voice and warm touch would creep into his conscience as he slept. It all seemed ages ago to Jihan. Dhuli, his father had a small plot of land and harvest from there provided for his small family of three. Valli, Jihan's mother had been the village belle and had fallen in love with Dhuli. However, five years after Jihan was born, she died under mysterious circumstances and her body was found near the village lake on the outskirts of the forest. Most of their neighbours said that she had been raped by the local landlord's son and killed. Dhuli went mad with rage and grief but his attempts for justice went futile. Some months thereafter he was beaten to death by the same landlord's son for touching the steps of a well that belonged to the landlord's family. Numbed and alone, Jihan continued with life with his old grandmother who had come from the neighbouring village to look after him and had stayed on.

Once, Jihan had sought education as the only means to escape this humiliating and sorrowful life. And at that juncture, he had met Kaaveri, who too, was striving to break free of the shackles of this unequal social system. Together, they would imagine the world of their togetherness, sitting on the outskirts of the forest, not far from where Jihan's mother's body had lain. In the third year of his engineering course, Kaaveri had come into his life, when she joined the college in his village and came to live with her maternal uncle's family. However, their friendship was disrupted when the landlord's grandson and his friends came to the village during the summer vacation. Not just Kaaveri but they would tease and assault any girl of the village. The villagers kept quiet and pushed their daughters further into the interior of the house, forbidding them from walking around in the village. Kaaveri was different. She opposed this move in the village panchayat and firmly called the offenders by their name stating that they should be punished instead of the village harassing and confining their own girls and women. Dheivamani, the landlord's grandson had started to plot her assault and murder from that day itself. Jihan took it upon himself to protect Kaaveri at each step and this was also his way of staying close to her. But that fateful night, the landlord's grandson with the help of his father had managed to threaten and persuade Aneesh Babu (on the pretext of killing his family) to take Jihan out of town for a day. Aneesh Babu had quietly followed the plan and taken Jihan with him but, barely 5km into the journey he started crying and said, "Jihan, go back to the village, this instant! They will kill Kaaveri, Save Her!" In disbelief, Jihan had stared at the bent over, fragile old man who kept nudging him amidst tears.

He jumped down from the bus, before it slowed down and ran towards his village. The sun was hovering over the horizon as he ran with only the thought of reaching Kaaveri. But as he neared the village, he heard only shrieks and cries, and his heart knew that the worst had happened. Kaaveri's bloodied, lifeless body was on the ground and Jihan, after taking a glance, slowly walked away. For twelve days he sat on the steps of his house, not speaking, having little food and sleeping on the porch. The villagers let him be, hoping that he would soon emerge from this period of mourning. On the thirteenth day, Tori, his neighbour, came running to him, "Aneesh Babu has committed suicide," he said.

Jihan did not flinch or respond in any way. He sat there till dusk, then got up and went to Dheivamani's house, filled with fire and fury. Dheivamani, seeing him, started with his usual stance of mocking him, but as he uttered the first sentence, Jihan landed a resounding blow on his head with an iron rod and Dheivamani lay sprawled on the floor, dead. Mayhem broke loose and not many were spared that night when Mrgam was born!

* * *

So many years had passed it seemed as dawn snuck in slowly and Jihan kept watching Akashi's anxious eyes. Those eyes that had stopped him, those eyes so much like Kaaveri's, those eyes he could not see closed, those eyes that brought him back to life, those eyes that reminded him of happier days and what he could have been. How could he kill those eyes? He knew he had to save her from Sambhu, who would ravage and then kill her. This time he could not let Kaaveri die! This time he would not be late.

Enclosed within the tall grass, Akashi had not felt the chill of the night. She sat wondering what her next step should be – she needed to look for the road, that was the only way to get help.

"What happened to the passengers of the bus," she wondered. "There was no sound throughout the night!"

A rustling sound alarmed her, as she watched intently. However, instead of any wild animal she found a tall, lean man, dressed in black shirt and pants, emerging. He had a brown blanket in his hand, which he tossed towards Akashi. "Take it!" a deep voice resounded.

Akashi was surprised, she had not expected to see a man in this forest speaking in English to her.

"Don't stereotype," she reminded herself. "Being a villager does not mean he will be illiterate."

He gestured to her to get up and follow him. Strangely, Akashi felt reassured and complied. While walking through the scattered brambles, she asked, "What is your name? Why are you helping me and where are we going?"

He replied quietly, "You can call me Mrgam."

"The Beast!"

"Why should I call you that?" she retorted.

"Why were you named so?"

He turned towards her. It was those same red piercing eyes that she had seen last night.

"Look! If you don't want to be killed, just keep quiet and follow me!"

"I am taking you to the nearest highway, from where you can get transport to the city!" he said in that same deep quiet voice.

Some time elapsed, Akashi had no idea how long it was, where they were, she simply followed out of fear and confusion. All her belongings including the phone was in that bus. She suddenly stopped and shouted to Jihan, "Mrgam, where is the bus? It must be nearby."

"What happened to them?"

"They ran away," he calmly replied.

"What! Leaving me!" Akashi was stupefied.

"You or the whole bus of passengers! I too would have gone with the bus!" he said. A small smile was forming on the side of his lips.

Almost two hours of walking Akashi had revealed her life story to this man who often asked her questions showing his interest in what she narrated.

However, now Akashi started becoming doubtful. "Where was the road?"

"Is he really trying to help me?"

Mrgam suddenly stopped and stretched out his arm protectively shielding Akashi. Some distance away, she saw a group of men walking towards them.

He quietly whispered to Akashi, "Take the left, that narrow passage will lead you to the highway!"

"Go, don't delay! Meanwhile I will stop them!" He held Akashi's hand, briefly, and nudged her in that direction.

Mrgam knew that once Sambhu had seen the girl, he would never let her go. He had to stop him. He would never let Sambhu touch her. After a long time, someone had spoken to him and seen him as a person. He would never let that be taken away.

He walked towards his gang. They were smiling at him. "What is that item you are bringing for us, early in the morning?" Sambhu asked with a smile. Smacking his lips, he kept looking at Akashi's direction.

"Sambhu, it's just a lost traveller. Let her go!" asserted Jihan.

"Mrgam, I am the leader, do not give orders to me!" retorted Sambhu.

Jihan looked at Akashi and nodded for her to go. Sambhu, seeing that, told his men to go behind her. But Jihan was not having any of it. He stopped the men and put up a fight. As Jihan shouted, "Run!" she never looked back. She kept running and soon the highway emerged in front of her. She knew Mrgam could not stop them for long. She frantically waved hands at any passing vehicle. Soon a bus stopped and as she looked back, she found Mrgam running behind two men who were headed in her direction. Shocked, she watched Sambhu point a gun at her. Precisely then Mrgam ran up in front of her and the bullet pierced his heart.

One of the passengers pulled her to the steps and the bus sped away. Akashi watched numbly as Mrgam fell on the ground, blood spattered everywhere and waving to her and shouting, "I am Jihan!"

Since that day Akashi had searched for Mrgam. He was never found.

* * *

Earlier that night Akashi had picked up a book from the seat above her. The driver had said, "The last passenger had forgotten it." She opened the first page of the book in the hopes of finding the name and address of the owner. The title stated Local Legends and she soon found herself staring at a sketch of Mrgam – half human, half beast – the same red eyes that were going to penetrate her soul staring right back at her!

THE WAY OF THE KAFTAR

BY SCOTT CHADDON

"Ambush! Murphy! Hit the dirt!" Anderson's warning blared through the tac radio. Seamus dropped to the ground as a burst of machine gun fire passed directly overhead. Glancing back at his unit, Seamus confirmed that all heads were going to be down until the gunfire ceased or paused. It was all the time he would need. The gunfire was coming from some ancient, low stone walls rising out of the sand, twenty meters northwest of their position. Leaping up, he sprinted toward the sniper. Two rounds impacted his left shoulder and one pierced his right thigh. Ignoring them, Seamus covered the distance to the enemy with blinding speed, kicking up a cloud of sand in his wake. The insurgent's eyes widened as Seamus leapt, clearing the five foot wall and, in a single, flawless motion, impaled him on his combat knife. The gunman released a weak cry as the blade was driven up into his chest, lifting him off of the ground and killing him instantly. Seamus flung the lifeless body against the nearest wall and sounded his signature wolf whistle. The unit rose to their feet almost as one, weapons at the ready, and advanced to Murphy's position. As the troops moved in, Murphy detected the scent of six other men who had also occupied the location but had departed within the last ten minutes.

"The unlucky bastard remained to cover the others' retreat," said Lieutenant Smythe as he nudged the corpse with a boot. "See these tracks here?" He pointed at footprints in the sand. "There were at least four others."

"Hot damn, Lucky!" exclaimed Simms with a laugh. "Still the best damn point man ever!" He clapped Seamus on the shoulder as Murphy scrubbed the gore from his hand and cleaned his knife.

"His aim sucked," Murphy lied. His shoulder and leg itched a little but the rounds had not even done enough damage to make him bleed. The other three members of his Advanced Reconnaissance Unit joined him, reporting that the immediate area was secure for the time being. The Lieutenant gave him the nod and Murphy gave them new orders. They dispersed to keep an eye out for movement while Lt. Smythe relayed the sitrep to command while the troops secured the perimeter.

Once the area was secure and sentries assigned to stand guard, the unit made camp and settled in. The next watch got some sack while the others went about their duties. At dinner Private Coleson, the green recruit, asked the inevitable question.

"Sarge, why is it they call you Lucky?" The rest of the soldiers within earshot laughed. Murphy knew he would not have to respond. Simms loved to recount the tales.

"Private, you're looking at the luckiest son of a bitch in the entire corps," laughed Simms. "Murphy there has seen more combat missions than any five of us combined, and he still has yet to take a single wound. This man has been to Hell and back and come through without a scratch!" Murphy could detect the scent of awe drifting off of the PFC. The Lieutenant cleared his throat, getting the attention of everyone present.

"Listen up men," said the Lieutenant. "We drew the short straw on this one. There's a village just south of As Samawah. It's a weapons depot and staging area. We've learned that they're going to assault our main column. Our mission is to take the village, secure or destroy the depot and deny the enemy this support. We will be engaging a larger, heavily armed force, so be prepared. We move out at first light."

"What does that mean?" There was a slight quiver in Coleson's voice.

"That means we're expected to suffer high casualties," said Simms. "So, get some sleep and be sure to check your gear and ammo." There was a muttering of agreement among the men. Murphy could scent worry in the platoon, and fear was rolling off of Coleson in clouds. Seamus and his team were assigned extended range night recon. Under the circumstances, long range recon was SOP, so they finished eating, grabbed a map each and headed out. Murphy directed his men to spread out and report in ten minute intervals.

Once out of sight, he stripped down, it would not do to completely destroy his clothes. Taking a deep breath, he concentrated, triggering the transformation. Murphy clenched his teeth to suppress his groans and growls of agony as bones twisted and lengthened, his skull reshaped into a canine muzzle, long canines pushed their way out. Long, dark, coarse hair burst from every inch of his skin. Joints and muscles expanded and stretched, adding height and weight to his already impressive size. The change never took more than forty seconds, but was so painful that it always felt like an hour. Once the transformation was complete, he burst into a full run. The moon provided him plenty of light to see by. Sand sprayed up behind him and dunes whipped past on either side as he ran. He covered the miles in minutes and soon had the target in sight. He panted lightly from the run as he assessed the situation. The report was gravely inaccurate. They were outnumbered six to one. If his unit challenged this force, it would be a meat grinder. He knew immediately what he had to do. There was no way he was going to allow his buddies to die in this place. Seamus moved in so quickly that they would not know what hit them. All they would see was a dark blur, and a flash of teeth and claws attached to an eight-foot-tall killing machine. He barely had to use his bite. Razor sharp talons, backed by muscles more powerful than twenty men, sliced through armor, flesh, and bone effortlessly. Six were dead and down before they even knew they had company. The body count had risen to fifteen by the time they could react. Blood and body parts flew everywhere, creating a deeper form of shock and awe than they were prepared for; Than anyone was prepared for. Knives and bullets had no more effect on him than their fists or curses. He shrugged them off easily, the sting of the wounds no more than a mild annoyance. Though a trio of the enemy had managed to escape the twenty minute blood bath, the terrified witnesses would be thought insane before they would be believed. Seamus was grateful that no military force on the planet could afford to issue silver bullets. Once everything was quiet, he piled the bodies around the munitions dump and, using gasoline, set them on fire. In the midst of the chaos and the clean-up, he never missed a check in.

Following a quick sand scrubbing, he collected his tac radio, sprinted back to his position and dressed. Murphy had resumed his assigned position moments before the depot exploded, lighting up the night, and filling the air with a thunderous blast. The gasoline had taken longer to set off the munitions than he had expected. Seamus signaled his team to return to camp. As secondary explosions could be heard in the distance, the Lieutenant ordered everyone up and, ten minutes later, the platoon was on its way toward the brightly burning column of flames. They stopped half a klik from their target to examine the situation. When no sign of the enemy was detected they moved in closer. Nothing had survived the explosions, blackened sand and bits of glass were all that remained.

"That crater used to be our mission," said the Lieutenant.

"Looks like we have a friend out there, Sir," said Williams; Simms high fived him.

"Not necessarily," he replied. "They have an enemy. That's not the same thing."

"What now, Lieutenant?" asked Seamus.

"I want your team to do a full recon of the site, while we provide cover. I want com checks every five minutes. When you return we transmit our sit rep and then move off to a safe distance to await further orders."

"Yes, Sir." He and his team departed for the burning ruins, the darkness granting them excellent camouflage. They circled the area and he crafted his report objectively, as if he had never been there before.

After reporting the incident, the platoon was ordered back to base camp. They were scheduled to remain on base for three weeks, on alert status. Simms, as usual, interpreted this as permission to throw a party. Murphy had no interest in parties or drinking, the last thing any of these men wanted was for him to lose his self-control. Instead, he volunteered for mobile guard duty so he could keep busy. Extra duty never hurt the paycheck either.

On the second night, he started picking up the scent of the local predators. Hyenas were viewed as a scourge by everyone, including the locals, who, despite this, refused to kill them. Minutes later, Murphy picked up a strange scent, even by hyena standards. Just one scent trail that smelled like, and unlike, a hyena. The scent seemed to be a strange mixture between hyena musk, human sweat, metal, and oil. There was no doubt in his mind that it was another shapeshifter, though not one he was familiar with. He filed the scent away in his mind and continued his patrol.

The next night, one of the guards was mauled to death. Doctors reported that the wounds had been inflicted by a hyena. Seamus chose to investigate the scene of the attack personally, and picked up the same, strange scent he had detected the night before. Knowing he could not explain what he had discovered to his superiors, he resolved to be even more vigilant than normal. Something strange was going on. Because he preferred night duty, the minor physical changes required to enhance his senses would go unnoticed. The extremely fine-tuned control over his ability to change had taken him more than nine decades to perfect.

On the third night, Murphy caught the scent on a cross wind and moved to intercept the owner before it could kill again. When he tracked it down, he was confused. The source of the scent was an Iraqi national, a small, naked man. Murphy's nose never lied. He narrowed his eyes and he leveled his weapon at the stranger.

"This is the property of the United States of America. Turn around and go back the way you came." The man started to laugh until Murphy chambered a round. He scrutinized Murphy and then sniffed at the air.

"What are you?" The Iraqi's English was heavily accented, his brow wrinkled curiously.

"I'm an American soldier," said Murphy. The small man dismissed the statement with a wave of his hand.

"No, no. What," he emphasized the word, "what are you?" He started smiling as he pointed a finger at Murphy. The finger stretched into a claw, and the man began to grow, and sprout hair, his eyes glowed golden and then red. Murphy swore under his breath as he discarded his rifle. He did not have silver bullets either. He pulled off his gear as the werehyena snarled and leapt at him.

Murphy managed enough of a change to catch the incoming monster by the throat and heave it a full fifteen meters away. He managed to kick off his boots and pants by the time it recovered and came charging back. Completing his own transformation, the hyena-man skidded to a stop as Murphy towered more than two feet taller. Seamus allowed a deep growl to rumble in his throat as his hackles rose. Doubt momentarily registered on the hyena-man's face before it recovered and attacked. The thing leapt up and latched onto his shoulder. The jaws were incredibly powerful. Murphy snarled as he caught one of the clawed hands and realized just how much stronger he was than his opponent. With a sudden twist, the were-hyena's arm snapped in three places, eliciting a high pitched cry of pain. Seamus plunged one of his claws into his enemy's back, breaking ribs and grabbing the spine between the shoulder blades. The creature finally released his shoulder with a scream of agony just as Murphy disemboweled him. The monster went limp and the light left its eyes. Seamus released him and dropped the body on the ground. To his surprise, the insurgent did not heal, instead he had died. What kind of lycanthrope was this? Murphy was not surprised when it began changing form. What stunned him was that its natural form was that of a hyena. He cleaned himself up, dressed again, and resumed his watch, his wounds disappearing quickly. Murphy had a lot to think about.

Another week passed without incident. His unit received their next assignment and they were on their way once again. Theirs was a combat heavy reconnaissance mission into the lands surrounding Karbala to assess the threat level of any surrounding cells of militants, and then eliminate them. The insurgents preferred to move at night. This meant that they were resting during the day, making them vulnerable. Unless there had been a sand storm, Seamus could track any scent trail. Any time he smelled gun metal and human sweat, he knew he had a live one. He was, naturally, careful to be ambiguous concerning the nature of the trails he would report.

In four days' time they had successfully eliminated six cells. On the morning of the fifth day, their orders changed. They were to begin night maneuvers and use night vision tech to identify the enemy. Some other unit had almost wiped out a group of refugees and Command wanted to avoid another such incident. Murphy did not need the goggles, his vision was better in the dark without them, but he still carried a pair in case the sky was overcast, or there was little or no moon to see by.

The first night out, Murphy crossed the scent trail of an entire hyena clan. He reported the animal trail and issued a warning. Their presence made him wary, and he pushed his senses to the limit. When he crossed another scent trail, he recognized the odors, it was the same clan. This time he detected the distinctive smell of the were-hyenas. Murphy loosened his clothes and gear and untied his boots so he could get out of them quickly at need. Thirty minutes after crossing the clan's trail for the third time, he started to see their eyes glowing golden in the darkness. He swore under his breath. There were at least sixty of them waiting for him, and every single one was a were-hyena. Murphy called the platoon to a halt, explaining that he had encountered a large pack of hyenas directly in their path. The Lieutenant instructed him to drive the animals away so they could continue. He confirmed that he would take care of it and would radio back when he was finished. Strangely, the hyenas just waited in the darkness. He quickly divested himself of his gear, piling it neatly before striding toward them and making a complete change into his hybrid form. The largest member of the clan made a kind of grunt and then, like a wave of hair, teeth and claws, they came for him.

Seamus allowed his feral nature some slack as he closed with the monsters and released a howl that made his opponents lose a step. With a snarl fueled by his primal and savage nature, Murphy gutted four of them with a single swipe of his claws. He waded into the enemy like a buzz saw. Hardly feeling the bites and claws, he ripped into them, savoring the ability to cut loose for the first time in over fifty years. Any pent up fury and frustrations he had, he took out on these creatures. Though he was bleeding from a score of wounds, the clan quickly decided that it had had enough and fled. He gave chase and killed six more before they had scattered too far for him to effectively follow. He released another howl from the core of his being, a warning to those that had fled.

He fought to regain control of himself one step at a time as he traced his own scent back to the battle site. He counted thirty-seven dead, including those he had chased down, easily half of their clan. As he scrubbed the blood and gore away, he remembered hearing a word being yelled over and over as the leader called out orders. As Murphy spent a few minutes packing bandages in his more severe wounds. He wondered what the word 'kaftar' meant. His deepest wounds would take less than an hour to heal, but he needed to stem the blood flow so he would not stain his uniform and raise questions. Healing took resources, so he consumed the five pounds of beef jerky in his pack along with both canteens of water. It was nothing like a fresh steak, but it would serve until chow time. Once his gear was back on, he switched on his radio and reported that he had used his private supply of jerky to provoke them into fighting each other. He warned them that there were a lot of dead animals in their path. The Lieutenant confirmed that they had heard the animals fighting. The hyena trails he came across afterward were strong with fear scent. He did not bother to report those. He hoped that that would be the last time he would see them. Much to his relief, the rest of the mission passed successfully without further incident from the hyena people.

While they were stopped at base camp between missions, Murphy tracked down one of the Marines' Iraqi translators, Rahim Abdallah, a round man with a pleasant demeanor. Murphy arrived while he was in the middle of a translation. An hour later, a young couple left. Not wanting to rush the man, he waited two minutes before going in. When he did, Mister Abdallah was preparing to leave.

"Mister Abdallah? Could I have a few moments of your time, Sir?"

"Ah, I am off to lunch."

"Please, Sir, I just need to know the meaning of a word."

"One word? Very well, this should not take long. What is it?" Abdallah smiled curiously.

"What does the word 'kaftar' mean?" Murphy was dead serious but Abdallah looked amused.

"Kaftar? Where did you hear this word?"

"I heard someone shouting it a couple of weeks ago. What does it mean?"

"This is a myth. The legends say that a kaftar is a shape-shifter that changes from hyena to man and back again. They are also believed to be, or belong to, witches and wizards. To kill one is a great taboo, one who slays a kaftar risks being cursed by its ghost, or by the witch or wizard who owns them."

"Witches and wizards?"

"Ah yes, they are humans who use magic to become a hyena. It is said that the kaftar are extremely loyal to their masters, even to the point of sacrificing themselves. Female kaftar, it is said, have the ability to hypnotize people. Stories say that they use this ability to manipulate humans into the darkness where they kill and eat them. Of course, the superstitious do not openly discuss the kaftar in public. They feel that even talking about them will bring misfortune."

"That's very interesting. Thank you."

"You are most welcome. Have a good day." The man smiled and departed. Murphy followed the translator out. At least he knew what they were called, and a little about the mythology. It was not a secret that they could be killed, though no Iraqi dared to slay one. He returned to his platoon to ponder this new information. Most people scoffed at the idea of magic and mythology. Being a werewolf, Murphy did not have the luxury of disbelief. His platoon had two weeks remaining at base camp and he spent it researching the subject online. There was remarkably little information available on the obscure shape shifters. It did not take long for that particular well to run dry.

The next mission sent them into the lands surrounding Diwaniyah. Intelligence had reported an active cell causing trouble around the city. The mission was to locate and, if possible, neutralize the cell. Their transport dropped them off two klicks outside of As Samawah. Diwaniyah was a major regional crossroads and, as such, was tactically important. Their platoon was one part of a combined effort to keep the crossroad open, and the insurgents suppressed.

On the second night of recon, Murphy had only just caught a whiff of the kaftar when Callum's voice came over the tac radio. He had begun to report movement, but was interrupted by animalistic growling followed by his screaming. The Lieutenant ordered the others to close on Callum's position. Scant moments later, Martin, and then Anderson, could be heard screaming in the distance, there was a brief burst of gunfire, and then silence. The platoon went into full defensive mode. That left only Murphy out in the dark. He was torn between grief and fury when six kaftar came into view, two were limping. They waited while he shed his clothes and gear. Why did they always wait? Murphy wondered as he turned off his tac radio. Why not just attack? It looked like Anderson had caused some damage before he went down. He changed and, when they closed in on him, he could smell the blood of his friends in their fur. He gave in to his fury.

Seamus launched himself at them. They looked surprised for a moment and then terrified as he ripped apart the first four to enter his reach. The last two managed to shatter glass bottles against him before they too fell. The bottles covered him with a pungent powder that made his skin tingle. Murphy's anger was nowhere near satisfied, but there were none left to kill. He decided, reluctantly, that he needed to return to his platoon. His anger transformed into alarm when he discovered that he could not change back! What had they done to him? His mind sobered, and then tumbled into the myth. It was a curse or a spell.

He had to think quickly! He switched his tac radio back on as he gathered his gear. He made the sounds of snarling and yelling into the radio, dropping it and his weapon in the sand before running off into the desert. Without a body, the Lieutenant would believe he had been captured or dragged off as prey. Three klicks out, he finished stuffing his clothes into his pack, picked up the trail of the kaftar and decided that it was time to carry the fight to them. If he could not rejoin his platoon, then he was free to inflict as much damage as he saw fit on this new enemy.

The kaftar had taken great steps to conceal their trail. Unfortunately for them, Murphy's senses and wits were too sharp. Two days later, he tracked the trail back to an uncharted oasis. He had had time to think as he tracked them. If they had attacked him with some kind of spell, he would need to rid himself of it. Knowing they were nocturnal, he approached during the day. Securing his pack high in a tree, he used the vantage point to get a general idea of the layout.

There were ten sentries guarding various tactical points, but they were not within easy sight of one another; easy pickings. One by one, he took them down without a sound. They never saw or heard him coming. This left the clan vulnerable. His first desire was to kill until none remained, but his training kicked in and he decided that a covert recon would be best to assess the threat and maximize effectiveness. As he slipped silently through the oasis, he counted groups and numbers, figuring that the largest group would include the wizard or witch. As he was doing this, he noticed that females and the young lived in hollows at the base of the largest trees. Inside these dens, there were two to four females and up to a dozen cubs. He decided to leave them be. No matter how angry he was, killing mothers and children was not his way. The men lived in small, stick huts or just rested out in the open. He discovered a single wooden structure in the oasis, a large shack. Murphy was certain that the leader must live there. He was no expert on magic, but every movie he had ever seen on the subject agreed that, if you kill the caster, you break the spell, so that was his primary target. There was no doubt in his mind that the place was trapped, so he would have to draw him out.

After completing his assessment, he discovered that, not counting mothers and cubs, he had already decimated three fifths of the clan. Dispatching sleeping kaftar was not the same as slaying humans, who slept much deeper. Seven of them had died before the alarm was sounded and chaos ensued. This time the kaftar fought with a surprising ferocity, some even sacrificed themselves so others could make a successful attack.

He did not doubt that this ferocity was because he had invaded their home. As he cut down his opponents he worked his way towards the shack. There was a moment when they had almost overwhelmed him, four weighted down each limb while others attacked relentlessly. He freed himself by catching one of his attackers in his jaws and flinging that kaftar into the group holding his right arm, sending them sprawling. It only took moments after that for him to free himself. He had taken several severe wounds to his abdomen, and did not dare open himself up like that again. He could heal almost anything as long as silver was not involved, but being eaten alive sounded pretty final to him.

When he had waded to within fifty meters of the shack he could see a human male, presumably the wizard, standing in the doorway, holding several glass bottles in the crook of one arm, the other hand cocked back and ready to throw. The closer Murphy moved toward the leader, the more furiously the kaftar fought to keep him away, but they did not possess the strength and their numbers were dwindling. When the bottles started flying, Murphy was prepared for it. As each bottle was hurled his way, he would either throw a kaftar into the path of the missile or use one for a shield. Those that got hit would either burst into flames or begin dissolving as if they had been doused in acid. The screams of agony were horrible. When the leader returned with another arm load of bottles, Seamus grabbed up a smallish kaftar and heaved him into the air right at the leader. There was a look of surprise on the Wizard's face just moments before the kaftar collided with him, knocking both of them inside the shack where Murphy could hear the sound of shattering glass, followed by a massive explosion that collapsed the building and caused it to burst into flames. The explosion drew the attention of every were-hyena, giving Murphy the opportunity to tear apart those kaftar within easy reach. Ten minutes later, the battle was over and dead kaftar littered the ground. It would be a while before the cubs were old enough to cause anyone trouble and by then, he hoped, the war, itself, would be over.

He limped over to the spring fed pool that was the oasis' water source, leaving the carnage behind to get fresh water and some rest. He tried to change back but nothing happened. His dismay blended with exhaustion and pain, so, after bathing and tending to his wounds, he lay by the pool and slept. When he finally woke up, hours had passed, night had fallen and all of his wounds had healed. He surveyed the battle site and found that the bodies had been piled on the burning shack and subsequently were reduced to ash. Who would have done that? Then he remembered about the adult females. He wondered why they had not attempted to kill him as he slept. Normally, this would have been a fatal error. Yet, they had left him undisturbed.

He went to retrieve his belongings and found them scattered all over the sand beneath the tree he had hidden them in. He caught the scent of kaftar cubs and sighed, shaking his head ruefully. Obviously, the curiosity and mischievousness of children was universal. He located his pack and gathered what he could. His rations, water, letters from home, and camping gear were nowhere to be found. What little he did find were mostly uniforms, and they were in rough shape. Murphy was forced to consider the idea that he may never return to America. After all, no one would transport him looking like this. He was still a United States Marine, even if he was stuck in this form, and he resolved that he would continue with his mission by eliminating the enemy. It was the only way he could think of to protect his unit. His map was not too badly damaged, so he made for those areas he knew were occupied by insurgents. He was intent on doing significant damage to their numbers and resources. Feeling somewhat responsible for the cubs, Murphy would bring back a couple of large animals after each raid for them to feed on. The meat seemed well received.

Two weeks later, he had eliminated ten enemy encampments and acquired a locally woven cloak of sorts. It was an earthy, sand color and he used it to camouflage himself during the day. After each mission, Murphy returned to the oasis to rest. The females, ten in all, completely avoided him. They would not meet his eyes when he did encounter them. The pups, twenty-seven by his count, played and romped and, at the mother's instruction, began learning to change into human form. It was fascinating. With the moon at its full and shining glory, Murphy sat by the pool and watched the pups play and eat his most recent catch. He fell asleep smiling.

When he awoke at sunrise, Murphy was thrilled to discover that he had returned to human form. He changed back and forth several times to be certain that he had complete control once again, then laughed aloud as he looked around. Not a single kaftar was within sight. He did not mind. It was time to return to his unit and his life. Without his tags, or any ID, it would be difficult, but not impossible. Murphy got a drink, dressed himself in the cloak, his torn up cargo pants, and boots. He left behind what remained of his gear to keep up appearances and ran sand through his hair, dusting himself and his clothes all over with it. With his disguise in place, he made his way to the nearest road and waited until a US Army transport approached. He staggered out onto the road and allowed them to 'rescue' him. He was taken to base camp to give his report and be debriefed twenty times by military intelligence.

During his walk to the road, he had conceived a simple story of his capture and escape. Murphy explained how the cell that had captured him was attacked by an unknown enemy. He managed to slip away in the confusion and had barely managed to scrape together enough food and water to survive, wandering the desert until he was able to find a place he recognized.

After two weeks in a hospital bed, being pampered, fed and rested in relative isolation, he was finally returned to his unit for a month before shipping out. He was awarded a bronze star for valor and was informed that he would be cycled home to receive therapy for his fictional PTSD. He did not like to lie, but if he just bounced back after what he had described, they would be suspicious, and suspicion was a dangerous thing.

Simms threw a party on his behalf and he got to meet the new SR team that had been sent to replace his. Seamus was asked by various members of his unit to retell his tale a dozen times before they sent him home to Texas. His parents had passed away decades before, leaving him the ranch that had been his safe haven growing up. He had enlisted a pair distant cousins to manage the place and supervise the ranch hands while he was overseas. Murphy knew that he was never going to be sent abroad again during this tour, though he still had two years left. He would spend his remaining time in counseling and teaching new recruits. He deplaned, hailed a taxi and checked in with his superiors before getting permission to go home. While he was not affected psychologically the same way that normal humans were, he was still in need of a long rest. When the taxi pulled up to the ranch, Tina and Robin, his cousins, came out to meet him and they were not happy. When he got out, he could scent Tina's panic and Robin's outrage. He paid the driver and shushed his cousins.

"Now, just one of you, tell me what the problem is." Murphy rubbed his temples.

"They arrived about two weeks ago," started Tina, "and all they'll say, is that they're yours. Their English leaves a lot to be desired."

"They? Who are 'they'?" Seamus was bewildered. "What do you mean by 'mine'?"

"Why didn't you tell us to expect them? We were caught completely off guard." Robin was miffed. "What were you doing over there, besides ten Iraqi women?"

"What? No! I didn't do anything like that." Murphy put a hand up and all talking stopped. "Okay, where are these people? We'll get this straightened out right now."

"Follow us." Tina led the way with her characteristic swagger. He trailed behind, lugging his bags. He could not imagine whoever it was they might be talking about. He had not dallied with one woman, much less ten! The doors opened and Seamus was stunned by what he saw. Ten Iraqi women and twenty-seven children were moving about the house doing chores or, in the children's case, playing. They stopped as soon as he entered the house. Seamus recognized each and every one of them by scent. The women gathered and settled the children. The entire group bowed at his feet as one. His cousins froze where they were and stared, wide eyed.

"Master," said the women in unison, their accents were very heavy indeed.

"Master," repeated the children as one. Tina and Robin turned and looked at him like he had grown a second head. Seamus could only shake his head as he pressed his fingertips to his temples. As he thought back to what he had learned about the kaftar and their ways, it made a kind of twisted sense. He sighed heavily, wondering how on earth they had managed to get here on their own.

"Yeah," he said with a sigh of resignation, "they're mine alright."

WILDCAT

BY CRIS MORRIS

P eter looked back. The shadow was still back there, somewhere. He could feel it. He saw no movement on the sidewalks, but there were several cars parked along the curb that would provide cover. At three in the morning, the city provided little sound as cover for heavy footsteps. It was those steps that first alerted Peter to someone following him. He reached into his front pocket, felt the weight of his pocketknife. It wasn't much, but the feel of having anything at all provided some sense of security.

He tried not to hurry, tried not to let whoever was following him know that he was panicked. He feared it would escalate the attack he expected any moment. He listened. There. There was the light echo of a hard-soled shoe hitting the concrete walk. He turned a corner and looked again toward the sound. A quick movement caught his eye before the side walk was hidden by the building. Yes, someone was back there for sure.

Peter eyed both sides of the street. "Come on," he said to himself, "there has to be somewhere I can go." The city slept around him – all of the shops were closed and shuttered, the people were asleep in their beds, safe from his stalker. He should have been in his room by now, sleeping soundly, and not worrying about someone following him.

*　*　*

"And then, she said, 'So much for a hole in one!'" The three men around him laughed, drawing glares from the other patrons. Peter smiled at the tasteless joke and sipped from his beer. His hand began to shake again, and he set the bottle down. He grabbed it with his free hand to keep it from falling over.

"You okay, Skipper?" Mark, seated across from him, leaned forward. "You look a little tipsy."

"I'm fine." He wasn't tipsy, as Mark suggested. The doctors called it 'essential tremors,' as if there was something necessary about them that he hadn't yet discovered. Medication helped, but never fully dulled the sensation. His health was not a topic for discussion, though, so let them think he was a little drunk.

Tom tossed a couple of pretzels into his mouth and chewed. He always chewed with his mouth open, often while trying to hold a conversation. It was repulsive. Peter tried to avoid talking to the man if food were around, but tonight was unavoidable.

Jarod, the fourth man at the table continued to chuckle. He put his head down to avoid everyone's eyes. His large belly shook. "Hole in one," he said and laughed again.

Tom stood, held his bottle high, and while still chewing on pretzel, bits of soft dough spritzing the table, "To closing the deal!" They all stood, clinked bottles, and drank. Peter had managed to hold himself to two beers tonight, a feat his wife, ex-wife, would have been shocked to see. The last doc had told him not to mix his meds with alcohol.

"Last call!" The bartender rang a bell at this pronounce-ment. Groans echoed from the dark corners of the bar.

"Last round is on the company," said Tom. He left the table to get their drinks. Peter glanced at his watch – ten minutes to one in the morning. He wiped a hand across his face and blinked. It had been a long day of negotiations, a successful day, and he was bone-tired. He also found it harder and harder to stay up late these days. On a normal night, he would have been in bed at least two hours ago.

A few minutes later, the four men, surrounded by the other patrons, spilled out onto the sidewalk. Tom – of course it'd be Tom, Peter thought – pointed down the street. "I know of a little hole in the wall that way." Without waiting for an answer, and not bothering to check if any of them followed him, Tom stumbled away. The other patrons had drifted away, going home, going to a different bar, who knew.

Jarod shrugged. "Might as well." He jogged after Tom.

"I suppose I should go along and make sure they stay out of trouble. You coming?"

Peter looked at Mark, said, "Not tonight. I'm exhausted. I think I'll crash at the hotel and see you in the morning."

Mark clapped on the shoulder. "Okay, Skipper. See you tomorrow." He smiled and walked away.

"I should have gone with them," said Peter. Somewhere along the way back to the hotel, he'd made a wrong turn and got lost. Soon after, he had picked up his shadow. Or, at least, he had become aware of his shadow. When had this person begun following him? Maybe it was one of the locals from the bar who had waited in hiding after last call? "Probably someone who saw me wandering around." He rubbed the pocketknife again.

He continued down the street, eyes swiveling back and forth, trying to locate some familiar landmark. Graffiti marked some of the walls now – "The End Is Nigh", "Jules Rules", "1-800-Eat-Shit", and other text gems. Peter stopped to admire the artistry of a few of the paintings. Most were dim in the low light, but the bright colors offset that. The skill of many of the paintings stunned him. He had left his phone back at the hotel room. Not for the first time this night, he wished he had it with him. Now, he would have used the camera to take photos of some of these works.

He was staring at a large painting of the Madonna on a two-story brick wall when the sound of clanging metal grabbed his attention. He turned around. Three young men leaned on a car across the street. All three were dressed in ratty jeans, t-shirts, and canvas shoes. Peter thought they looked around twenty years old and resembled one another enough that they might be brothers. One smoked a cigarette, one crossed his arms, and the third tapped an aluminum bat against the car's front hubcap.

"Admiring the sites, are we?" said the smoker.

He put his hand in his pocket and felt the knife again. His left hand had begun to shake again, so he stuffed it into his other pocket, hoping to hide it. He tried to smile, hoped it didn't look too nervous, and nodded. "Beautiful painting. One of yours?"

"Nah, man, not us," said the man with crossed arms.

"We wouldn't do that," said the bat holder.

Peter swallowed. "No, of course not."

"What," said smoker, "you think we're not good enough?" The other two laughed. Peter did not like the sound of it.

He held his hands up. "No, no, not at all."

Bat boy stood. He tapped the bat against the road and the ping echoed back from the buildings. Peter took a step back.

Smoker dropped his cigarette and stomped it out. Crossed arms stood and put his hands in his pockets.

"I don't want any trouble, fellas."

Smoker laughed and started across the street. The others followed him. Peter backed down the sidewalk the way he'd come.

"Toss us your wallet and your phone, and you won't have any." Crossed arms pulled a switchblade from his pocket and swung it open with a practiced flick.

"I... I don't have my phone." Peter reached into his back pocket and retrieved his wallet. He pulled the twelve dollars he had out and set them on the ground. "This is all of the money I have." He took another step back and ran into something solid. A hand fell on his shoulder. He glanced back, knowing it had to be his shadow.

A large man, over six feet tall with long black hair past his shoulders, stood behind him. He was older than the three, but not by much. "I don't think they believe you." The man's voice was deep and Peter could feel it rumble through the hand on him. "Let's open it up and take a look, yes?" Peter's hand began to shake again. "Don't be scared," the man said, "we won't kill you. We'll hurt you a little, sure, but only as much as you make us."

Peter gritted his teeth and tried to stop the shaking. He felt a warmth spreading up from his feet. His blood pounded in his ears. His mouth fell open at the sight of his hands. Thick, yellow fur began to coat them. His fingers shortened, but the nails elongated and narrowed into claws.

"What?" Smoker had picked up the few dollars before they could blow away and now looked up at Peter. "What are you?"

The man behind him stepped back. Peter heard a rending sound, but couldn't place its source. Bat boy stepped up and cocked the bat back over his shoulder. The wallet fell from

Peter's paws. The night was bright as day now and he could hear the mens' breathing, their heartbeats.

The bat swung at his head. He saw that the boy swung for all he was worth, but the bat seemed to take its time getting to him. Peter swiped at the bat. He felt resistance for a moment as his claws dug into the metal. The bat fell into two pieces with a loud screech and Peter's swing continued across the man's throat. The man fell backward, his bat forgotten, and grasped his bleeding neck with both hands. Peter smelled death on the man, and turned away from him.

The other three threw themselves at him. The next few minutes were loud with roars, with screams, with the thuds of falling bodies. Soon, Peter stood alone in the middle of the street. He was on four feet instead of his usual two, and the perspective confused him.

Peter swung round at a sound behind him. He knew this was his shadow, could smell the man coming, recognized his face, but leaped at him anyway.

Peter slammed into a parked car. The man was fast. Peter hadn't seen him move. He was strong, too. Peter shook his head and turned back to the man. A grizzly bear stood before him, but it had the same smell as the man. He charged, but was knocked aside again.

The bear seemed to have no interest in attacking him while he was down. He circled the bear, looked for an opening. The bear turned with him, but offered no weakness. Peter charged again. The bear grabbed him from the air, spun him round, and pulled him in tight. His back was to the bear's belly, but he hissed and clawed and tried to reach it.

"Peter, stop." He knew that voice. He stopped swinging at the bear, but his fur was still raised and he continued to hiss. "Peter, it's me, Tom." He glanced back as best he could. The bear was gone and he was held in the grip of his co-worker, a grip that was nearly as strong as the bear's had been. "I'm going to set you down." Tom dropped him to the ground.

Peter spun and hissed again. Tom stood, hands out, much as he had done with the three young men by the car. Peter backed up until he was against a car. He sat down and licked the blood from one paw. His eyes never left the man. As he calmed, Peter felt the transformation begin again, but in reverse this time. Soon, he shivered in the cold. His clothes were in tatters by the sidewalk – the rending he had heard earlier. Tom was squatted down beside him, also nude.

"You're quite the wildcat, Peter." Tom laughed. "I suspected you were one of us, and I'm glad to see that I was right."

"I don't understand. What's happening to me?" Peter sobbed.

"It's okay, Peter. It can be a little disorienting at first."

"I'm cold. I need clothes." He looked Tom up and down. "We need clothes."

"I know a place a couple of blocks from here. We can get clothes, a stiff drink, and I can explain it all. Do you think you can walk that far?"

Peter thought a moment. He appeared to be uninjured. He nodded.

"Good." Tom stood and reached out a hand. Peter took it and Tom pulled him to his feet. "Follow me." Tom walked back the way they had come, scooped his clothes on the way. He did not seem to care that he was exposed to anyone who might be awake. Peter looked around, surprised that no one was looking from a window to see what the racket had been.

He gathered his own belongings, stepped over the headless corpse of the large man that had come up from behind him, and followed Tom.

* * *

The two men, dressed in warm clothes, sat at a small plastic table and nursed brandies in small glasses. Peter stared at his hands. They were steady. He was surprised at this, sure that they would be shaking from the adrenaline, or trauma, or something.

"I think you can stop taking your meds now, Peter."

He looked up. "What?"

"The shaking? That's how I recognized you. It's a common symptom leading up to transformation."

"Oh." He looked back down at his glass.

Tom lit a cigarette. He offered one to Peter, but he shook his head no. "Okay, Peter," Tom leaned forward on his elbows, "here is what you need to know. You are a lycanthrope, a shape-shifter. In your case, you are werepanther. Me," he cocked a thumb at himself, "I'm a werebear."

"Uh huh."

"I know, I know. It's hard to believe, but it's true. You felt it, you saw it. You saw the aftermath of it with those four pieces of trash that you took out."

"I killed them." Peter drank. He closed his eyes, focused on the burn in his throat when he swallowed.

"You did. And rightly so. They wouldn't have amounted to anything in this world."

"I killed them." He looked up at Tom. "They were thugs, sure, but they were still living, breathing human beings, and I killed them."

Tom smiled. "Yes. They were human beings, not lycan-thropes like us."

"What do you mean?" Peter set his glass down and leaned back.

Tom sat back up as well. "It means you are superior. We're better than humans. We're faster. We're stronger."

"But, I was human until tonight." Peter blinked away tears.

Tom reached across the table and touched his hand. "No, Peter, you weren't. You looked human, of course. You acted human because that is all you had been taught. But you have always been much more than that. You didn't know it until tonight." He pulled his hand back. "Tonight, you were born again, my friend."

Peter sighed and sipped from his glass again. "How did this happen? I never wanted to hurt anyone, to kill anyone. I wanted to do my job and to be left alone." He took a deep breath. "I have to go to the police. I have to tell them what happened."

Tom shook his head. "And what happened, Peter? What happened that they would possibly believe. You'll tell that they attacked you so you turned into a cougar and killed them all? Is that it?" He leaned forward again. "No, Peter, there is nothing you can tell them that they will understand and no reason to tell them anything."

"I can't pretend it didn't happen, Tom."

"Nor should you. It was your first time. You will transform many times before you grow old. You will kill again." He waved his hand around the room. "It may be an accident, it may be self-defense like tonight, and it may be because you realize you are superior and that humans are meant to submit to us."

"I don't feel superior."

"I can introduce you to many more like us. There are dozens of us in this city alone. We can have a get-together, a little barbecue, or something. You can get to know them. Once you do, you will see and understand."

* * *

"So, this Peter?" The tall man with white hair shook his hand. He was their host, a Mr. O'Connell. Tom had told him the man had made a fortune in the steel business. Peter had to look up at him. "Welcome to my home." He let go of Peter's hand. "And thank you for bringing him Tom."

"My duty and my pleasure," said Tom. Peter glanced side-eyed at him. Tom was being friendly to everyone here, but the Tom he knew, the one who told ribauld jokes and talked with his mouth full, was absent. Mr. O'Connell walked away to greet other guests.

Peter adjusted his bow tie. "Not exactly what I had in mind when you said barbecue, Tom." Tom clapped him on the shoulder and laughed.

Peter sipped from his champagne glass and eyed the room. In all, about twenty people were in attendance. Tom had introduced him to most of them. They were politicians, business leaders, professors, and lawmakers. All of them were Lycanthropes. Peter could hear the capital on that word anytime anyone spoke it aloud. He was a glorified salesman at his company. How could he be in the same room as these people? However, everyone seemed to know Tom and to genuinely like him. Everyone also seemed to know him. Peter felt exposed, but drew some comfort from Tom's presence, something he never would have expected.

Hours later, when the party was beginning to disperse, Peter had changed his mind. The people were friendly toward him. None of them looked down on him due to his position. He had even received job offers and was considering more than one of them. Tom, it seemed, was where he needed to be. He was in a position to keep an eye out for 'new talent' as they called it. He did not receive any offers of which Peter was aware, nor did he seem to care.

"What do you think?" Tom was at his elbow once again.

"Perhaps it's four glasses of champagne talking, but I think I can feel at home here."

"Good to hear, my friend."

"I still don't feel superior to humans as you put it, but I feel equal to those at this party. They are all likable people." He set his empty glass down on a table. "I met Elizabeth Bartholomew, the actress." Tom smiled. "I couldn't believe it was her, Tom. She talked to me like she'd known me for years. I was speechless at first. I mean, who wouldn't be in the presence of such beauty, but by the time we parted, she had given me her personal number." He grinned. "Me. I have her number, Tom."

"That's great Peter. I knew you'd come around. Now, our host would like a word before we leave." He touched Peter's elbow.

"Sure, sure." He allowed Tom to guide him.

"I trust our little soirée was to your liking, Peter?"

"Yes, sir, Mr. O'Connell. I had a lovely evening. Thank you for having me."

"Will we be seeing more of you, perhaps?"

Peter held out his hand and the tall man took it. Peter shook. "I hope so."

Mr. O'Connell smiled. "In that case, Peter, welcome to the TRG."

BIOGRAPHIES

Ben White is the author of The Buddha Bastinado Blues, The Kill Gene, Conley Bottom: A Poemoir, The Recon Trilogy +1, Say Their Names (Under Anonymous), and Always Ready: Poems from a Life in the US Coast Guard. He also has had short stories, essays, and poems published in various journals. However, he has lived in the world of Cure as Kali Metis' editor.

Dr. Keith Raymond is a Family and Emergency Physician. He practiced in eight countries in four languages. Currently living in Austria with his wife. When not volunteering his practice skills, he is writing, lecturing, or scuba diving. In 2008, he discovered the wreck of a Bulgarian freighter in the Black Sea. He has multiple medical citations, along with publications in Flash Fiction Magazine, The Grief Diaries, The Examined Life Journal, The Satirist, Chicago Literati, Blood Moon Rising, Saddlebag Dispatches, Utopia Science Fiction magazine, and in the Sci-Fi anthologies Sanctuary and Alien Dimensions among others. He is the fiction editor of SavagePlanets magazine.

Scott Chaddon is a published sci-fi, fantasy, and horror writer. His stories have appeared in several anthologies: Occult Detective Monster Hunter: A Grimoir of Eldrich Inquests Volume 1, Building Red: Mission Mars, Explorer One, The

Dead Game, COLP: Black and Gray, Gypsum Sound Jails, Spirit Walker, Santa Claws is Coming to Deathlehem, and Red Cape Publishing A-Z Anthology of Horror: Q for Quantum, S for Slasher, and T for Tarot. He has also been published in several magazines: The Last Line Journal, Sci Phi Journal, Wingless Dreamer, and Eastern Iowa Review.

Katie Ness is a published poet with Hecate Magazine, Mulberry Literary, The C Word Magazine, Beyond the Veil Press, Poetry Cove and others. Her essays, articles and magickal musings feature in Femme Occulte, Witches Magazine, Kindred Spirit Magazine, Witchology, and more. She has two poetry books published, the first is Aphrodite Fever Dream published with Undressed Society Press and Juggernaut published with DarkThirtyPoetry Press.

Katie thrives along quirky edges, roving with the rippling rhythms of shadows and light that we call life. She has a BA Hons in Fine Art and has diplomas in the Anthropology of Ritual & Magic and Archeology of the British Isles and Sicily. Her MA is forthcoming. Katie is a Hedgewitch and Priestess– of which her practice involves ceremonies with deities, ancestors & spirits. She lives in London but travels extensively– often exploring sacred sites across Britain and abroad. Her short story collection and mystical travel essays are being worked on over copious amounts of tea. Katie is of French, Mediterranean and Romani ancestry on her mother's side.

She studies Roma folklore.
https://www.instagram.com/katie_wild_witch/

Trevor Abbud is an up-and-coming author in speculative fiction and an ardent fan of thrillers and meaningful narratives. He discovered his passion for writing at a young age.

Embracing this passion, he transitioned into writing with a serious commitment. Trevor, a devoted family man raising four kids, finds inspiration in the picturesque surroundings of the New Jersey bayside where he resides. His captivating tales serve as thrilling entertainment and a cathartic release, helping him navigate and channel his experiences with mental health challenges. With a penchant for crafting stories that resonate with depth and meaning, Trevor's short stories and poems have found homes in publications such as Nat 1 Publishing, GNU Journal, Foliate Oak Literary Magazine, Chantwood Magazine, The Broke Bohemian, Seshat Magazine, and The Hungry Chimera. Currently immersed in crafting his second novel, Trevor continues using his writing as a powerful tool for self-expression and connection with readers.

Deborah Brennan is a journalist for Cal Matters and Voice of San Diego. She has written about politics, environment and a little of everything else for newspapers including the San Diego Union Tribune, Los Angeles Times, Los Angeles Daily News and various magazines. When she's not covering political intrigue, she has walked the eery shores of the Salton Sea, tracked sea turtles in San Diego Bay and dove into kelp forests off the California coast. She lives in North County San Diego and employed the region's beaches and backcountry for her "INCURABLE" story about the collision between the worlds of lycanthropes and selkies.

Jerry Purdon writes dark fantasy and horror stories. Earlier works include "Bottom Drawer", "Beer in a Bar" and "Grave-yard Game." "Monster" is due out in the summer of 2025 in an annual short story anthology due by Running Wild Press. Jerry spends a fair amount of time grilling and loves a great bowl of chili. His favorite activity is to sit outdoors engrossed in a great book. He holds a B.A. in Literature from University of Houston - Clear Lake. He is married to his ideal reader and lives in Texas where he creates his stories seared in terror.

Cris Morris lives in Houston, TX. By day, he is absorbed in writing computer software. In his free time, he writes horror involving monsters.

When trying not to be obsessed about the right knife for the job, **Patrick Scott** enjoys the way a nice piece of rested meat slices. It's because he cooks, not anything too dark. He allows his spirit of competition to come forth when playing cutthroat games of Splendor and Ticket to Ride and the ever-challenging Ticket to Ride Europe. He's told stories for a long time, is never without a notebook and is known to drop out of conversation when something magical captures his heart and mind. Patrick published his debut novel, *Big Beasts*, in 2020. *Unburied*, the first book in the *Loci of Power Series*, arrived in 2022. Both series live at Atmosphere Press. Get in touch with Patrick at patrickscottbooks.com.

Christopher Pender lives in Galway City which is known as the City of the Tribes, in the wild and beautiful west coast of Ireland. Ireland is a beautiful country with a rich history and culture. Chris is married with two beautiful children. He has studied Theology and Philosophy, writing his final dissertation on Saint Patrick who is the patron saint of Ireland.

He was brought up on old Irish folk tales which in turn he has passed on to my own children. Writing has always been a beloved hobby. However, in time he began to take writing more seriously, submitting his work to magazines and publishers. For Chris, writing is an intellectual, emotional and spiritual experience, creating new worlds and characters to inhabit them. It is a satisfying experience to see his work in print. It means that he can share my innermost ideas with other like-minded people, including fellow authors and readers - a wonderful, vibrant and supportive community of which he is proud to be a part of.

Dr. Neepa Sarkar's collaborative monograph will be soon published by IBIDEM Press. She has a Ph. D in English Literature and has taught in the Department of English, Mount Carmel College, Bengaluru and has been published in History Today, Middle West Review, Irish Studies Review, The Confidential Clerk, Mejo Journal, Journal of Literature and Aesthetics, Glocal Colloquies, De Gruyter Press and Lexington Books, Within and Without Magazine, Curious Blue Press, Shot Glass Journal (Muse-pie Press- Jan 2024), Wingless Dreamer Publications, Cyberwit publishers, Daath Voyage journal, Metonym Journal (Spring 2024), Anodyne Magazine (Spring 2024) and Shiuli Magazine.

Find her work here:
https://filmsliteratureandphilosophy.wordpress.com/

ABOUT RUNNING WILD PRESS

Running Wild Press publishes stories that cross genres with great stories and writing. RIZE publishes great genre stories written by people of color and by authors who identify with other marginalized groups. Our team consists of:

Lisa Diane Kastner, Founder and Executive Editor
Cody Sisco, Acquisitions Editor, RIZE
Benjamin White, Acquisition Editor, Running Wild
Peter A. Wright, Acquisition Editor, Running Wild
Resa Alboher, Editor
Angela Andrews, Editor
Sandra Bush, Editor
Ashley Crantas, Editor
Rebecca Dimyan, Editor
Abigail Efird, Editor
Aimee Hardy, Editor
Henry L. Herz, Editor
Cecilia Kennedy, Editor
Barbara Lockwood, Editor

Scott Schultz, Editor
Rod Gilley, Editor

Evangeline Estropia, Product Manager
Kimberly Ligutan, Product Manager
Lara Macaione, Marketing Director
Joelle Mitchell, Licensing and Strategy Lead
Pulp Art Studios, Cover Design
Standout Books, Interior Design
Polgarus Studios, Interior Design

Learn more about us and our stories at www.runningwild-press.com

Loved these stories and want more? Follow us at runningwildpublishing.com, www.facebook.com/runningwild-press, on Twitter @lisadkastner @RunWildBooks

RUNNING WILD

RUNNING WILD PRESS

NOTES

THE SUMMER OF SLIGHT ACQUAINTANCES

1. 'irunda mrgam' in Tamil refers to a dark beast.